THE **ATRIA** INTERNATIONAL BOOK OF MYSTERIES

THE
ATRIA
INTERNATIONAL BOOK OF
MYSTERIES

Your Passport to a World of Murder and Mayhem

ATRIA BOOKS

WASHINGTON SQUARE PRESS

EMILY BESTLER BOOKS

New York · London · Toronto · Sydney · New Delhi

Divisions of Simon & Schuster, Inc.
1230 Avenue of the Americas
New York, NY 10020

First Atria Books edition March 2012

ATRIA BOOKS/EMILY BESTLER BOOKS /WASHINGTON SQUARE PRESS and colophons are trademarks of Simon & Schuster, Inc.

For information about special discounts for bulk purchases, please contact Simon & Schuster Special Sales at 1-866-506-1949 or business@simonandschuster.com.

The Simon & Schuster Speakers Bureau can bring authors to your live event. For more information or to book an event, contact the Simon & Schuster Speakers Bureau at 1-866-248-3049 or visit our website at www.simonspeakers.com.

Manufactured in the United States of America

10 9 8 7 6 5 4 3 2 1

ISBN 978-1-4516-7663-1
ISBN 978-1-4516-7665-5 (ebook)

CONTENTS

Publisher's Note   vii

Collecting Cooper BY PAUL CLEAVE   1

The Burning Soul BY JOHN CONNOLLY   13

Burned BY THOMAS ENGER   25

Midwinter Blood BY MONS KALLENTOFT   39

Shunning Sarah BY JULIE KRAMER   51

Northwest Angle BY WILLIAM KENT KRUEGER   61

Last Will BY LIZA MARKLUND   75

Devil in a Blue Dress BY WALTER MOSLEY   97

Blessed Are the Dead BY MALLA NUNN   113

Unwanted BY KRISTINA OHLSSON   127

Dog on It BY SPENCER QUINN   149

The Book of Lost Fragrances BY M. J. ROSE   159

The Goat Woman of Largo Bay BY GILLIAN ROYES   173

CONTENTS

A Double Death on the Black Isle BY A. D. SCOTT   181

South by Southeast BY BLAIR UNDERWOOD,
    TANANARIVE DUE, AND STEVEN BARNES   195

About Atria Books   211
About Emily Bestler Books   213
About Washington Square Press   215

Dear Readers,

In all corners of the world and throughout time, from modern-day Jamaica and Sweden, to 1950s Scotland and Zimbabwe, through ancient Egypt, there's a mystery to be solved. And, there's a hero to solve it.

Within this sampler, you'll encounter such heroes. There's the father who is desperate to find out who killed his son in a terrible fire; the wise, loveable, and intensely loyal canine who works alongside a down-on-his-luck private investigator; the former sheriff of Tamarack County, a family man who has seen too much; and so many more.

Keep reading to learn about them all, and get a taste for their adventures throughout the world. We hope you enjoy the excerpts that follow. They have been carefully curated to give you a sense of our ongoing series—after all, once you find a character who you admire, there's nothing more satisfying than getting to read all of their adventures.

If you would like to learn more about any of our authors, please visit us at atria-books.com, follow @atriabooks, or like us at facebook.com/atriabooks.

Best,

Judith Curr

ALSO BY PAUL CLEAVE

Blood Men

Cemetery Lake

The Killing Hour

The Cleaner

COLLECTING COOPER

by Paul Cleave

Introducing Theodore Tate

Four years ago, Christchurch police detective Theodore Tate was a contented man with a wife and daughter who gave him a work/life balance hard to come by for most people in his line of work, until an accident killed his daughter and left his wife with permanent brain damage. Now Tate is the definition of a man down on his luck. A recovering alcoholic and just released from a four-month prison stint for having caused a DUI accident and nearly killing a young woman the same age his daughter would have been had she lived, he's finding it hard to maintain his once healthy sense of humor. It also doesn't help that apparently all of Christchurch's shadiest characters have been awaiting his return. A tough guy who feels deep sympathy for anyone touched by violence, Theodore Tate has never had to search for the dark heart of the city he loves, nor the darkness in the hearts of men. They follow him like shadows.

——————

Read on for a look at the first chapter of Paul Cleave's
Collecting Cooper **where you will meet Theodore Tate.**

Currently available as a paperback and eBook from **ATRIA** BOOKS

New Zealand

The dust from the exercise yard clings to the hot air. Flies and mosquitoes are trying to use my neck as a landing strip. Giant concrete walls separate me from the sounds coming from the other side where men are ticking through life, kicking a football or playing cards or getting stomped on. Cranes and scaffolding are off to the right, workmen creating additions to a prison that can't keep up, dirt and cement dust hugging the air like an early winter's fog, so thick the details are hard to make out, could be a stampede of cows just came through, could be a stampede of prisoners are trying to escape. My clothes smell stale and feel stiff; they've been folded and jammed inside a paper bag for the last four months, but they're sure as hell more comfortable than the prison jumpsuit I worked, slept, and ate in. Sweat and confinement is still on my skin. Heat is radiating up from the blacktop pavement into my feet. When I close my hands, I can feel the metal and concrete walls that would isolate me from the world the same way an amputee can feel a phantom leg. My last four months have been all about isolation. Not just from the world, but from other prisoners too. I've spent day after day surrounded by cells full of pedophiles and other pieces of human trash that couldn't be thrown into the general population for fear of having their throats ripped open. Four months that felt like four years, but it could have been worse. I could have had my teeth smashed out and made to play fetch-the-soap every night. I was an ex-cop in a concrete-and-steel world surrounded by men who hated cops more than they hated each other. I felt nauseous being surrounded by child molesters, but it was the better alternative. Mostly they kept to themselves, spending their days fantasizing about what it was that got them arrested. Fantasizing about getting back to that life.

The prison guards watch me from the entrance. They seem worried I'm going to try and break back in. I feel like a character in a movie; that lost guy who wakes up in a different time and has to grab somebody by the shoulders to ask them for the date, including the year, only to be looked at like they're a fool. Of course I know the date. I've been waiting for this day ever since I got thrown inside. My clothes are a little bigger because I'm a little smaller. Prison nutrition is malnutrition.

The nine o'clock sun is beating down and forming a long shadow behind me. In most directions it looks like there is water resting on the surface of the ground, a thin pool shimmering in the heat. The blacktop grabs at the soles of my shoes as I walk across it. I have to hold my hand up to my face to shield my eyes. I've been out of jail for twenty-five seconds and I don't remember a day as hot as this before going in. I haven't seen much sun over the last four months and already my pale skin is starting to burn. The longer I was trapped behind those walls behind me, the further away this particular Wednesday seemed. Prison has a way of fooling with time. There are a few cars around belonging to visitors, and one has a guy leaning against it staring at me. He's wearing tan pants and there are dark rings in the armpits of his white shirt and he's lost a bit of weight since the last time I saw him, but the buzz-cut hair is still the same, and so is his expression, of which, lately, he seems to have only the one. I can smell smoke from something big burning far off in the distance. I close my eyes against the sun and let it warm my skin, and then burn, and when I open them again, Schroder is no longer leaning against the car. He's covered half the distance between us.

"Good to see you, Tate," Schroder says, and I take his hand when he reaches me. It's hot and sweaty and it's the first hand I've shaken in a long time, but I can remember how it goes. The prison food didn't rot all of my brain away. "How was it?"

"How do you think it was?" I ask, letting go.

"Yeah. Well. I guess," Schroder says, summing things up. He's just looking for words and not finding them, and Schroder won't be the last. A couple of exhausted-looking birds fly low past us, looking for somewhere cooler. "I thought you could do with a lift home."

There's a white minivan waiting near the entrance, the bottom half of it covered in dirt, the top half only marginally better. There're a couple of other guys released today sitting onboard, both have shaved heads and tattoo raindrops streaming from their eyes, they're on opposite sides of the van staring out opposite windows wanting nothing to do with each other. Another guy, a short, powerfully built man with all the fingers on his right hand missing, turning his fist into a club, is swaggering out from the prison, his arms puffed out to the side to encompass his large chest and even larger ego. He stares at me before climbing into the back of the van. I give it a week tops before they're all back in here.

Four of us are getting released today and I wasn't thrilled about the prospect of spending twenty minutes in a vehicle with any of them. I'm not exactly thrilled about spending time with Schroder either.

"I appreciate it," I tell him.

We head over to his dark gray unmarked police car that's covered in dust from the drive out here, making all the letters on the side of the tires stand out. I climb in and it's hotter inside. I play around with the air-conditioning and get some of the vents pointing in my direction. I watch Christchurch Prison get smaller in the side mirror before disappearing behind a large belt of trees. We hit the highway and turn right, toward the city. We drive past long paddocks with dry grass and barbed-wire fences. There are guys in those fields driving tractors and whipping up clouds of dirt and wiping the early-morning sweat from their faces. Away from all the construction and the air is clear.

"Any thoughts to what you're gonna do now?" Schroder asks.

"Why? You want to offer me my old job back?"

"Yeah, that'd go down well."

"Then I'll become a farmer. Looks like a pretty nice lifestyle."

"I don't know any farmers, Tate, but I'm pretty sure you'd make the worst kind."

"Yeah? What kind is that?"

He doesn't answer. He's thinking I'd make the kind of farmer who'd shoot any cattle being mean to the other cattle. I try to imagine myself driving one of those tractors seven days a week and moving cows from one field to another, but no matter how hard I try I can't get any of those images to stick. Traffic gets thicker the closer we get to town.

"Look, Tate, I've been doing some thinking, and I'm starting to see things a little different now."

"What kind of different?"

"This city. Society, I don't know. What is it you say about Christchurch?"

"It's broken," I answer, and it's true.

"Yeah. It's seems like it's been breaking down for a while. But things . . . things are, I don't know. It's like things just aren't getting better. You're out of the loop since leaving the force three years ago, but we're outnumbered. People are disappearing. Men and women leave for work or home and just never show up."

"My guess is they've had enough and are escaping," I suggest.

"It's not that."

"This is your idea of small talk?"

"You'd rather tell me about your last four months?"

We pass a field where two farmers are burning off rubbish, most of it bush that's been cut back, thick black smoke spiraling straight up into the sky where it hangs like a rain cloud without any breeze to help it on its way. The farmers are standing next to tractors, their hands on their hips as they watch, the air around them hazy with the heat. The smell comes through the air vents and Schroder shuts them down and the car gets warmer. Then we're heading past a gray brick wall about two meters high with

Christchurch written across it, no *welcome to* in front of the name. In fact, somebody has spray-painted a line through *church* and written *help us*. Cars are speeding in each direction, everybody in a hurry to be somewhere. Schroder switches the air-conditioning back on. We reach the first big intersection since leaving jail and sit at a red light opposite a service station where a four-wheel drive has backed into one of the pumps and forced all the staff to stand around in a circle with no idea what to do next. The board out front tells me petrol has gone up by ten percent since I've been gone. I figure the temperature is up about forty percent and the crime rate up by fifty. Christchurch is all about statistics; ninety percent of them bad. One entire side of the petrol station has been covered in graffiti.

The light turns green and nobody moves for about ten seconds because the guy up front is arguing on his cell phone. I keep waiting for the car tires to melt. We both get lost in our own thoughts until Schroder breaks the silence. "Point is, Tate, this city is changing. We catch one bad guy and two more take his place. It's escalating, Tate, spiraling out of control."

"It's been spiraling for a while, Carl. Way before I ever left the force."

"Well, these days it seems worse."

"Why am I getting a bad feeling about this?" I ask.

"About what?"

"About why you came to pick me up. You want something, Carl, so just spit it out."

He drums his fingers on the steering wheel and gazes straight ahead, his eyes locked on the traffic. White light bounces off every smooth surface and it's becoming harder to see a damn thing. I'm worried by the time I make it home my eyeballs will have liquefied. "In the backseat," he says. "There's a file you need to take a look at."

"I don't need to do anything except put on some sunglasses. Got some spares?"

"No. Just take a look."

"Whatever it is you want, Carl, it's something that I don't want."

"I want to get another killer off the streets. You're telling me you don't want that?"

"That's a shitty comment."

"See, the man I knew a year ago would have wanted that. He would have asked me how he could have helped. That man a year ago, he would have been giving me his help even if I didn't want it. You remember that, Tate? You remember that man? Or did those four months in the slammer fog up your memory?"

"I remember it perfectly. I remember you shutting me down when I knew more than you did."

"Jesus, Tate, you have a strange perception of reality. You got in the way of an investigation, you stole, you lied to me, and you were a real pain in the ass. Reality saw you kill somebody, it saw you crash your car into a teenage girl and put her in the hospital."

Last year I tracked down a serial killer, and people died in the process. Bad people. At the time I didn't know one of them was bad, and killing him was an accident. That guilt, it changed me. It got me drinking. And drinking led to the car accident which led to me getting sober again.

"You don't need to lecture me on reality," I say, thinking about my daughter, cold in the ground for three years and never coming back, then thinking about my wife in her care home, her body nothing more than a shell inside of which used to live the most perfect woman in the world.

"You're right," he says. "You're the last person who needs a lecture on reality."

"Anyway, I'm a different man now."

"Why, did you find God while you were locked away?"

"God doesn't even know that place exits," I tell him.

"Look, Tate, we're losing a battle and I need your help. That man a year ago, he didn't care about boundaries. He did what needed to be done. He didn't care about consequences. He didn't care about the law. I'm not asking any of that from you now. I'm only asking for your help. For your insight. How can a man who did all of that last year not want to offer that?"

"Because that man ended up in jail with nobody to give a damn about him," I say, the words more bitter than I intend them to be.

"No, Tate, that man ended up in jail because he got drunk and almost killed somebody with his car. Come on, all I'm asking is for you to take a look at the file. Read it over and tell me what you think. I'm not asking you to track anybody down or get your hands dirty. Truth is we're all losing perspective, we're too close—and hell, no matter what you've done or the actions you've taken, this is what you're good at. This is why you were put on this earth."

"You're stretching," I tell him.

"And trying to appeal to your ego." He takes his eyes off the road for a second to flash me a smile. "But what isn't a stretch is the fact that you can do with the money."

"Money? What, the police department is going to put me back on the payroll? I seriously doubt that."

"That's not what I said. Look, there's a reward. Three months ago it was fifty thousand dollars. Now it's two hundred thousand. It goes to whoever can offer information that leads to an arrest. What else you going to do, Tate? At least take a look at the file. Give yourself a chance to—"

His cell phone rings. He doesn't finish his sentence. He reaches for it and doesn't say much, just listens, and I don't need to hear any of the conversation to know it's bad news. When I was a cop nobody ever rang to give me good news. Nobody ever rang to thank me for catching a criminal, to buy me some pizza and beer and say *good job*. Schroder slows a little as he drives, his hand tight on the wheel. He has to swerve out wide to avoid a large puddle of safety glass from a recent accident, each piece reflecting the sunlight like a diamond. I think about the money, and what I could do with it. I stare out the window and watch a pair of surveyors in yellow reflective vests measuring the street, planning on cutting it up in the near future to widen it or narrow it or just to keep the city's roadworking budget ticking over. Schroder indicates and pulls over and somebody honks at us and gives the finger. Schroder keeps talking as he does a U-turn. I think about the man I was a year ago, but I don't want to be him anymore. Schroder hangs up.

"Sorry to do this to you, Tate, but something's come up. I can't take you home. I'll drop you off in town. Is that okay?"

"Do I have a choice?"

"You got any money for a taxi?"

"What do you think?" I actually had fifty dollars stuffed into my pants pocket for this day, but between the time I took my clothes off four months ago and got them back, that fifty found a new home.

We hit the edge of town. We get caught in thick traffic where a lane has been closed down so some large trees overlapping the power lines can be trimmed back, the trucks and equipment blocking the way, but the workers are all sitting in the shade too hot to work. We reach the police station in town. He pulls in through the gates. There's a patrol car ahead of us with two cops dragging a man out from the backseat, he's screaming at them and trying to bite them and the two cops both look like they want to put him down like a rabid dog. Schroder digs into his pocket and hands me thirty dollars. "This will get you home," he says.

"I'll walk," I say, and open up the car door.

"Come on, Tate, take the money."

"Don't worry—it's not that I'm pissed at you. I've been locked up for so long I need the exercise."

"You try walking home in this heat and you're a dead man."

I don't want his help. Problem is the heat is already close to blistering the paintwork on the car. It blasts through the open door, passing over my skin and sucking away any moisture. Even my eyes feel like they're being lubricated by sand. I take the money. "I'll pay you back."

"You can pay me back by picking up the file."

"No," I say, but I can feel it back there, pulling at me, this magnet for violence whispering to me, telling me within its covers is a map which will take me back into that world. "I can't. I mean . . . I just can't."

"Come on, Tate. What the hell are you going to do? You've got a wife to take care of. A mortgage. You've had no income for four months. You're slipping behind. You need a job. You need this job. I need you to take this job. Who the hell else is going to hire you for anything? Look, Tate, you nailed a serial killer last year, but do you think anybody is going to care about that? No matter how you justify it, or weigh up the rights and wrongs of what you did, the fact is always going to be the same—you're an ex-con now. You can't escape that. Your life isn't the same life it was back then."

"Thanks for the ride, Carl. It was about halfway useful."

It isn't until I'm on the street with the gates to the police parking lot closing behind me that I look down at the file, pages of death crammed inside its covers, waiting for me, knowing all along I couldn't turn it away.

———————

The story continues in *Collecting Cooper,* available in paperback and eBook from ATRIA BOOKS.

ALSO BY JOHN CONNOLLY

The Charlie Parker Stories

Every Dead Thing

Dark Hollow

The Killing Kind

The White Road

The Reflecting Eye (novella in the Nocturnes collection)

The Black Angel

The Unquiet

The Reapers

The Lovers

The Whisperers

Other Fiction

Bad Men

Nocturnes

The Book of Lost Things

The Samuel Johnson Stories
(for young adults)

The Gates

The Infernals

THE BURNING SOUL

by John Connolly

Introducing Private Investigator Charlie Parker

Private Investigator Charlie "Bird" Parker is a man seeking redemption. Tormented by the gruesome, unsolved murders of his wife and daughter, he is unable to escape his guilt and grief. Everything is questioned in Parker's mind; he obsessively wonders about the details of each case he takes on, turning them this way and that, believing that even the most obscure and unlikely element could lead to a breakthrough. Haunted by the ghosts of his wife and daughter, Parker knows firsthand of the darkness in men's hearts. The resolution of each case is a testament to his passion, fearlessness, and relentless pursuit of justice.

Step into the world of Private Investigator Charlie Parker with the first chapter of John Connolly's *The Burning Soul*, set in wintry Maine.

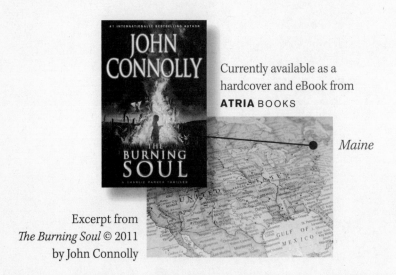

Currently available as a hardcover and eBook from
ATRIA BOOKS

Maine

Excerpt from
The Burning Soul © 2011
by John Connolly

Gray sea, gray sky, but fire in the woods and the trees aflame. No heat, no smoke, but still the forests burned, crowning with red and yellow and orange; a cold conflagration with the coming of fall, and the leaves resignedly descending. There was mortality in the air, borne on the first hint of winter breezes, the threatening chill of them, and the animals prepared for the coming snows. The foraging had begun, the filling of bellies for leaner times. Hunger would make the more vulnerable creatures take risks in order to feed, and the predators would be waiting. Black spiders squatted at the corners of their webs, not yet slumbering. There were still stray insects to be had, and further trophies to be added to their collections of withered husks. Winter coats grew thick, and fur began to lighten, the better to blend in against the snow. Contrails of geese arrowed the skies like refugees fleeing a coming conflict, abandoning those forced to stay and face what was to come.

The ravens were motionless. Many of their far-northern brethren had headed south to escape the worst of the winter, but not these birds. They were huge yet sleek, their eyes bright with an alien intelligence. Some on this remote road had noticed them already, and if they had company on their walks, or in their automobiles, they commented on the presence of the birds. Yes, it was agreed, they were larger than the usual ravens, and perhaps, too, they brought with them a sense of discomfort, these hunched beings, these patient, treacherous scouts. They were perched deep among the branches of an ancient oak, an organism approaching the end of its days, its leaves falling earlier each year, so that by the end of every September it was already bare, a charred thing amid the flames, as though the all-consuming fire had already had its way with it, leaving behind only the smoke smudges of long-abandoned nests. The tree stood at the edge of a small copse that jutted slightly at this place to follow the curvature of the road, with the oak as its farthest point. Once there were others like it, but the men who built the road had cut them down many years before. It was now alone of its kind, and soon it too would be gone.

But the ravens had come to it, for the ravens liked dying things.

The smaller birds fled their company, and regarded the intruders warily from the cover of evergreen foliage. They had silenced the woods behind them. They radiated threat: the stillness of them, their claws curled upon the branches, the bladelike sharpness of their beaks. They were stalkers, watchers, waiting for the hunt to begin. The ravens were so statuesque, so immobile, that they might have been mistaken for misshapen outcroppings of the tree itself, tumorous growths upon its bark. It was unusual to see so many together, for ravens are not social birds; a pair, yes, but not six, not like this, not without food in sight.

Walk on, walk on. Leave them behind, but not before casting one last anxious glance at them, for to see them was to be reminded of what it is to be pursued, to be tracked from above while the hunters follow remorselessly. That is what ravens do; they lead the wolves to their prey, and take a portion of the spoils as payment for their labors. You want them to move. You want them to leave. Even the common raven was somehow disturbing, but these were not common ravens. No, these were most uncommon birds. Darkness was approaching, and still they waited. They might almost have been slumbering were it not for the way the fading light caught the blackness of their eyes, and how they captured the early moon when the clouds broke, imprisoning its image within themselves.

A short-tailed weasel emerged from the rotted stump that was her home and tested the air. Its brown fur was already altering, the darkness growing out of it, the mammal becoming a ghost of itself. She had been aware of the birds for some time, but she was hungry and anxious to feed. Her litter had dispersed, and she would not breed again until the new year. Her nest was lined with mouse fur for insulation, but the little larder in which she had stored her surplus of slain rodents was now empty. The weasel had to eat forty percent of her own body weight each day in order to survive. That was about four mice a day, but the animals had been scarce on her regular routes.

The ravens seemed to ignore her appearance, but the weasel was too shrewd to risk her life on the absence of movement. She turned herself so that she was facing into her nest, and used her black-tipped tail as bait to see if the birds were tempted to strike. If they did, they would miss her body in aiming for her tail and she would retreat to the safety of the stump, but the ravens did not react. The weasel's nose twitched. Suddenly there was sound, and light. Headlights bathed the ravens, and now their heads moved, following the beams. The weasel, torn between fright and hunger, allowed her belly to choose. She disappeared into the woods while the ravens were distracted, and was soon lost from sight.

The car wound its way along the road, traveling faster than was wise and taking the bends more widely than it should, for it was hard to see vehicles approaching from the opposite direction, and a traveler unfamiliar with this route might easily have found himself in a head-on collision, or tearing a path through the bushes that lined the road. He might, were this the kind of road that travelers took, but few visitors came here. The town absorbed their impact, the apparent dullness of it dissuading further investigation, then spat them back the way they came, over the bridge and toward Route 1, there to continue north to the border, or south to the highway and on to Augusta and Portland, the big cities, the places that the peninsula's residents strove so hard to avoid. So no tourists, but strangers sometimes paused here on their life's journey, and after a time, if they proved suitable, the peninsula would find a place for them, and they would become part of a community with its back to the land and its face set hard against the sea.

There were many such communities in this state; they attracted those who wished to escape, those who sought the protection of the frontier, for this was still an edge state with boundaries of wood and sea. Some chose the anonymity of the

forests, where the wind in the trees made a sound like the breaking of waves upon the shore, an echo of the ocean's song to the
east. But here, in this place, there were forest *and* sea; there were
rocks ringing the inlet, and a narrow causeway that paralleled
the bridge linking the mainland and those who had chosen to
set themselves apart from it; there was a town with a single main
street, and enough money to fund a small police department.
The peninsula was large, with a scattered population beyond the
cluster of buildings around Main Street. Also, for administrative
and geographic reasons long forgotten, the township of Pastor's
Bay stretched across the causeway and west to the mainland.
For years the county sheriff policed Pastor's Bay until the town
looked at its budget and decided that not only could it afford its
own force, it might actually save money in the process, and so
the Pastor's Bay Police Department was born.

But when locals spoke of Pastor's Bay it was the peninsula
to which they were referring, and the police were *their* police.
Outsiders often referred to it as "the island," even though it was
not an island because of the natural connector to the mainland,
although it was the bridge that received the most traffic. It was
wide enough to take a decent two-lane road, and high enough
to avoid any risk of the community being entirely cut off in
foul weather, although there were times when the waves rose
and washed over the road, and a stone cross on the mainland
side attested to the former presence on this earth of one Maylock Wheeler, who was washed away in 1997 while walking
his dog, Kaya. The dog survived, and was adopted by a couple

on the mainland, for Maylock Wheeler had been a bachelor of the most pronounced sort. But the dog kept trying to return to the island, as those who are born of such places often will, and eventually the couple gave up trying to hold on to it, and it was taken in by Grover Corneau, who was the chief of police at the time. It remained with Grover until his retirement, and a week separated the deaths of the dog and its owner. A photograph of them together remained on the wall of the Pastor's Bay Police Department. It made Kurt Allan, Grover's replacement, wonder if he also should acquire a dog, but Allan lived alone, and was not used to animals.

It was Allan's car that now passed beneath the old oak and pulled up before the house across the road. He looked to the west and shielded his eyes against the last of the setting sun, bisected by the horizon. There were more cars coming. He had told the others to follow. The woman would need them. Detectives from the Maine State Police were also on their way following the confirmation of the AMBER Alert, and the National Crime Information Center had automatically been notified of a missing child. A decision would be made within the coming hours on whether to seek further assistance from the FBI.

The house was a ranch-style dwelling, neatly kept and freshly painted. The fallen leaves had been raked and added to a compost pile at the sheltered side of the building. For a woman without a man to help her, a woman not of this place, she had managed well, he thought.

And the ravens watched as Allan knocked on the door, and

the door opened, and words were spoken, and he stepped inside, and there was no sound or movement from within for a time. Two more cars arrived. From the first vehicle stepped an elderly man with a worn leather physician's bag. The other was driven by a woman of late middle age wearing a blue overcoat that caught in the car door as she rushed to the house. It tore, but she did not stop to examine the damage after wrenching it free. There were more important matters to which to attend.

The new arrivals had come together and were halfway across the yard when the front door opened wide and a woman ran toward them. She was in her late thirties, carrying a little weight on her waist and her thighs, her hair flying loose behind her. They stopped suddenly at the sight of her, and the middle-aged woman raised her arms as though expecting the other to fall into her embrace, but instead the younger woman pushed her way past them, jostling the doctor, one of her shoes falling from her foot, and the white stones on the drive tore at her skin so that she left smears of blood across them. She stumbled and landed heavily, and when she rose again her jeans were ripped, and her knees were scratched, and one of her fingernails was broken. Kurt Allan appeared in the doorway, but the woman was already on the road and her hands were at her mouth and she screamed a name over and over and over . . .

"Anna! Anna! Anna!"

She was crying now, and she wanted to run, but the road curved to the right and to the left, and she did not know which way to turn. The middle-aged woman came to her and wrapped her in her arms at last, even as her charge fought against her, and the doctor and Allan were approaching as she screamed the name again. Birds took flight from the surrounding trees, and unseen creatures burst from brush and scrub as though to carry the message.

The girl is gone, the girl is gone.

Only the ravens remained. The sun was at last swallowed by the horizon, and true darkness began to fall. The ravens became part of it, absorbed by it and absorbing it in turn, for their blackness was deeper than any night.

Eventually the weasel returned. The fat corpse of a field mouse hung limply in her jaws, and she could taste its blood in her mouth. It was all that she could do not to tear it apart as soon as she had killed it, but her instincts told her to control her urges. Her self-restraint was rewarded, though, for a smaller mouse had crossed her path as she returned to her home, and she fed on that instead before hiding its remains. Perhaps she would retrieve them later, once her larger prize was safely stored away.

She did not hear the raven's approach. Her first awareness of it came with the impact of its talons upon her back, tearing through her coat and into her flesh. It pinned her to the ground, then slowly began to peck at her, its long beak carving neat holes in her body. The raven did not feed upon her. It simply tortured her to death, taking its time over her agonies. When it had reduced her to a mess of blood and fur, it left the corpse for the scavengers and rejoined its companions. They were waiting for the hunt to begin, and they were curious about the hunter who was to come.

No, the one who had sent them was curious about him, and they watched on his behalf.

For he was the greatest predator of them all.

———————

The story continues in *The Burning Soul,* available in hardcover and eBook from **ATRIA** BOOKS.

COMING SOON FROM THOMAS ENGER

Pierced (October 2012)

BURNED

by Thomas Enger

Introducing Henning Juul

A house fire killed his six-year-old son and scarred his face for life. His marriage crumbled in the wake of the tragedy, and the seasoned investigative reporter took months to return to his job at a prestigious newspaper. But now he's back on the job, and the grisly murder of a young college student will test him in ways he's never expected. Henning Juul is world-weary and embattled, and the search for the killer—as well as his desire to unlock the mystery behind the fire that killed his son—drives him to face danger, threats on his life, and extraordinary risks.

—————

Read on for a look at Thomas Enger's *Burned* where you will meet Henning Juul just as he's returning to work after the fire that changed his life forever.

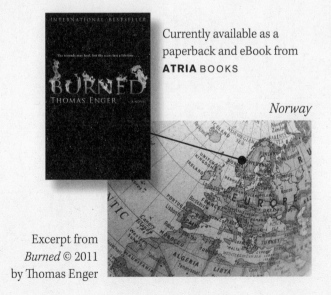

Currently available as a
paperback and eBook from
ATRIA BOOKS

Norway

Excerpt from
Burned © 2011
by Thomas Enger

He turns over with a disappointed grunt when his alarm clock goes off. He was halfway through a dream which evaporates as his eyes glide open and the dawn seeps in. There was a woman in the dream. He doesn't remember what she looked like, but he knows she was the Woman of his Dreams.

Henning swears, then he sits up and looks around. His eyes stop at the pill jars and the matchbox that greet him every morning. He sighs, swings his legs out of bed, and thinks that today, today is the day he'll do it.

He exhales, rubs his face, and starts with the simplest task. The pills are chalky and fiendish. As usual, he swallows them dry because it's harder that way. He forces them down his throat, gulps, and waits for them to disappear down his digestive tract and do the job that Dr. Helge enthusiastically claims is for Henning's own good.

He slams the jar unnecessarily hard against the bedside table, as if to wake himself up. He snatches the matchbox. Slowly, he slides it open and looks at its contents. Twenty wooden soldiers from hell. He takes one out, studies the sulfur, a red cap of concentrated evil. *Safety Matches* it says on the front.

A contradiction in terms.

He presses the thin matchstick against the side of the box and is about to strike it when his hands seize up. He concentrates, mobilizing all his strength in his hands, in his fingers, but the aggravating splinter of wood simply refuses to shift, it fails to obey and remains unimpressed. He starts to sweat, his chest tightens, he tries to breathe, but it's no good. He makes a second attempt, takes out another tiny sword of evil and attacks the matchbox with it, but soon realizes that he doesn't have the same fighting spirit this time, nowhere near the same willpower now, and he gives up trying to turn thought into action. He remembers that he needs to breathe and suppresses the urge to scream.

It's very early in the morning. That explains it. Arne, who lives upstairs, might still be asleep despite his habit of reciting Halldis Moren Vesaas's poetry day and night.

Henning sighs and carefully returns the matchbox to the exact same spot on the bedside table. Gently, he runs his hands over his face. He touches the patches where the skin is different, softer, but not as smooth. The scars on the outside are nothing compared to the ones on the inside, he thinks, and then he gets up.

The sleeping city. That's where he wants to be. And he is here now. In the Grünerløkka district of Oslo, early in the morning, before the city explodes into action, before the pavement cafés fill up, before mum and dad have to go to work, the children are off to nursery, and cyclists run as many red lights as they can as they hurtle down Toftesgate. Only a few people are up and about, as are the ever-scavenging pigeons.

He passes the fountain on Olaf Ryes Square and listens to the sound of the water. He is good at listening. And he is good at identifying sounds. He imagines there is no sound but the trickling water and pretends it's the day the world ends. If he concentrates, he can hear cautious strings, then a dark cello slowly intermingling before fading away and gradually giving way to kettledrums warning of the misery that is to come.

Today, however, he doesn't have time to let the music of the morning overwhelm him. He is on his way to work. The very thought turns his legs to jelly. He doesn't know if Henning Juul still exists, the Juul who used to get four job offers a year, who made the mute sing, who made the days start earlier—just for him—because he was stalking his prey and needed the light.

He knows who he was.

Does Halldis have a poem for someone like me, he wonders? Probably.

Halldis has a poem for everyone.

He stops when he sees the yellow brick colossus at the top of Urtegata. People think the huge Securitas logo on the wall means the security firm occupies the entire office block, but several private businesses and public bodies are located here. As is www.123nyheter.no, where Henning works, an Internet-only newspaper which advertises itself with the slogan "1–2–3 News—as easy as 1–2–3!"

He doesn't think it's a particularly good slogan—not that he cares. They have been good to him, given him time to recover, time to get his head straight.

A three-meter-tall fence with black metal spears surrounds the building. The gate is an integral part of the fence and slowly slides open to let out a Loomis security van. He passes a small, deserted guard booth and tries to open the entrance door. It refuses. He peers through the glass door. No one around. He presses a brushed steel button with a plate saying RECEPTION above it. A brusque female voice calls out "yes."

"Hello," he says, clearing his throat. "Would you let me in, please?"

"Who are you meeting?"

"I work here."

A period of silence follows.

"Did you forget your swipecard?"

He frowns. What swipecard?

"No, I haven't got one."

"Everyone has a swipecard."

"Not me."

Another silence. He waits for a continuation which never comes. "Would you let me in, please?"

A shrill buzzing sound makes him jump. The door whirrs. Clumsily, he pulls it open, enters, and checks the ceiling. His eyes quickly identify a smoke alarm. He waits until it flashes green.

The gray slate floor is new. Looking around, he realizes that many things have changed. There are big plants in even bigger pots on the floor, the walls have been painted white and decorated with artwork he doesn't understand. They have a canteen now, he sees, to the left behind a glass door. The reception is opposite it, also behind a glass door. He opens it and enters. There is a smoke alarm in the ceiling. Good!

Behind the counter, the woman with red hair in a ponytail looks fraught. She is frantically hammering away at the keyboard. The light from the monitor reflects in her grumpy face. Behind her are pigeonholes overflowing with papers, leaflets, parcels, and packages. A TV screen, hooked up to a PC, is mounted on the wall. The newspaper's front page clamors for his attention and he reads the headline:

WOMAN FOUND DEAD

Then he reads the strap line:

**Woman found dead in tent on Ekeberg Common.
Police suspect murder.**

He knows the news desk has yet to cover the story, because the title and the strap line contain the same information. No reporters have been at the scene, either. The story is accompanied by an archive photo of police tape cordoning off a totally different location.

Neat.

Henning waits for the receptionist to notice him. She doesn't. He moves closer and says hello. At last, she looks up.

First, she stares at him as if he had struck her. Then the inevitable reaction. Her jaw drops, her eyes takes it in—his face, the burns, the scars. They aren't large, not embarrassingly large, but large enough for people to stare just that little bit too long.

"It looks like I need a swipecard," he says with as much politeness as he can muster. She is still staring at him, but forces herself to snap out of the bubble she has sought refuge inside. She starts rummaging through some papers.

"Eh, yes. Eh, What's your name?"

"Henning Juul."

She freezes and then she looks up again, slowly this time. An eternity passes before she says:

"Oh, that's you."

He nods, embarrassed. She opens a drawer, riffles though more papers until she finds a plastic cover and a swipecard.

"You'll have to have a temporary pass. It takes time to make a new one and it needs to be registered with the booth outside before you can open the gate yourself, and, well, you know. The code is 1221. Should be easy to remember."

She hands him the swipecard.

"And I'll need to take your picture."

He looks at her.

"My picture?"

"Yes. For the swipecard. And for your byline in the paper. Let's kill two birds with one stone, right? Ha-ha."

She attempts a smile, but her lips tremble slightly.

"I've done a photography course," she says as if to preempt any protest. "You just stand there and I'll do the rest."

A camera appears from behind the counter. It is mounted on a tripod. She cranks it up. Henning doesn't know where to look, so he gazes into the distance.

"That's good. Try to smile!"

Smile. He can't remember the last time he did that. She clicks three times in quick succession.

"Great! I'm Sølvi," she says and offers him her hand over the counter. He takes it. Soft, lovely skin. He can't remember the last time he felt soft, lovely skin against his. She squeezes his hand, exerting just the right amount of pressure. He looks at her and lets go.

As he turns to leave, he wonders if she noticed the smile which almost formed on his lips.

*   *   *

Henning has to swipe his shiny new card no less than three times, going from the reception area to the second floor. Though the office is where it always was, there is nothing to remind him of the place he had almost settled into, nearly two years ago. Everything is new, even the carpet. There are gray and white surfaces, a kitchenette, and he would bet good money that there are clean glasses and mugs in the cupboards. There are flat screens everywhere, on the desks and on the walls.

He checks out the room. Four smoke alarms. Two foam extinguishers, possibly more. Good! Or good enough.

It is a large, L-shaped room. Workstations by the windows, tables and chairs behind colored glass partitions. There are tiny individual cubicles for when you want to conduct an interview without an audience or any background noise. There are lavatories, for the disabled as well, even though he can't actually see anyone even mildly infirm. He imagines there are rules about such things. They have always had a coffeemaker, but now they have the state-of-the-art version, which takes twenty-nine seconds to make a fancy cup of black coffee. Not four, like the old one.

Henning loves coffee. You're not a proper reporter unless you love coffee.

He recognizes the buzz immediately. Foreign TV stations, all reporting the same news over and over. Everything is *breaking news*. Stock exchange figures scroll along the bottom of the screen. A collage of TV screens show what NRK and TV2 are reporting on their strangely antiquated but still viable text TV pages. The news channel runs its features on a loop. It, too, has a ticker which condenses a story into one sentence. He hears the familiar crackle of a police radio, as if R2D2 from the Star Wars movies intermittently makes contact from a galaxy far, far away. NRK News 24 can just about be heard from a radio somewhere.

Bleary-eyed reporters tap on keyboards, telephones ring, stories are debated, angles suggested. In a corner by the news desk, where every story is weighed, measured, rejected, applauded, polished, or heavily edited, lies a mountain of newspapers—new and old—which the newly arrived reporters seize upon while they sip their first coffee of the day.

It is the usual controlled chaos. And yet everything seems alien. The ease he felt after years of working in the streets, of being *in the field,* of showing up at a crime scene, knowing he was in his element, has completely disappeared. It all belongs to another lifetime, another era.

He feels like a cub reporter again. Or as if he is taking part in a play where he has been cast as The Victim, the poor soul everyone has to take care of, help back on his feet. And even though he hasn't spoken a single word to anyone, except Sølvi, his intuition tells him no one thinks it's going to work. Henning Juul will never be the same again.

He takes a few, hesitant steps and looks around to see if he recognizes anyone. It's all faces and fragments from a distant past, like an episode of *This Is Your Life*. Then he spots Kåre.

Kåre Hjeltland is looking over the shoulder of a reporter at the news desk. Kåre is the news editor at 123news. He is a short, skinny man with messy hair and a passion which exceeds anything Henning has ever known. Kåre is the Energizer bunny on speed with a hundred stories in his head at any given time and an arsenal of possible angles for practically anything.

That's why he is the news editor. If it had been up to Kåre, he would have been in charge of every department and worked as the night duty editor as well. He has Tourette's syndrome, not the easiest condition to manage when you're trying to run a news desk and have a social life.

However, despite his tics and various other symptoms, Kåre pulls it off. Henning doesn't know how, but Kåre pulls it off.

Kåre has noticed him, too. He waves and holds up one finger. Henning nods and waits patiently, while Kåre issues instructions to the reporter.

"And stress that in the introduction. That's the hook, no one cares that the tent was white or bought from Maxbo last March. Get it?"

"Maxbo doesn't sell tents."

"Whatever. You know what I mean. And mention that she was found naked as soon as possible. It's important. It plants a sexy image in people's minds. Gives them something to get off on."

The reporter nods. Kåre slaps him on the shoulder and bounces toward Henning. He nearly trips over a cable running across the floor, but carries on regardless. Even though he is only a few meters away now, he shouts.

"Henning! Good to see you again! Welcome back!"

Kåre extends a hand, but doesn't wait for Henning to offer him his. He simply grabs Henning's hand and shakes it. Henning's forehead feels hot.

"So . . . how are things? You ready to chase Web hits again?"

Henning thinks earmuffs might be a good investment.

"Well, I'm here, that's a start."

"Super! Fantastic! We need people like you, people who know how to give the public what they want. Great! Sex sells, coffers swell! Tits and ass bring in the cash!"

Kåre laughs out loud. His face starts to twitch, but he carries on all the same. Kåre has coined a lot of rhyming slogans in his time. Kåre loves rhymes.

"Ahem, I thought you could sit over there with the rest of the team."

Kåre takes Henning by the arm and leads him past a red-glass partition. Six computers, three on opposite sides of a square table, are backed up against each other. A mountain of newspapers lies on a round table behind it.

"You may have noticed that things have changed, but I haven't touched your workstation. It's exactly the same. After what happened, I thought that you, eh, would want to decide for yourself if there was anything you wanted to throw out."

"Throw out?"

"Yes. Or reorganize. Or . . . you know."

Henning looks around.

"Where are the others?"

"Who?"

"The rest of the team?"

"Buggered if I know, lazy sods. Oh yes, Heidi is here. Heidi Kjus. She's around somewhere. In charge of national news now, she is."

Henning feels his chest tighten. Heidi Kjus.

Heidi was one of the first temps from the Oslo School of Journalism he hired a million years ago. Newly qualified journalists are usually so bursting with theory that they have forgotten what really makes a good reporter: charming manners and common sense. If you're curious by nature and don't allow yourself to be fobbed off with the first thing people tell you, you'll go far. But if you want to be a star reporter, you also need to be a bit of a bastard, throw caution to the wind and have enough fire in your belly to go the distance, accept adversity, and never give up if you smell a good story.

Heidi Kjus had all of the above. From day one. On top of that, she had a hunger Henning had never seen before. Right from the start, no story was too small or too big, and it wasn't long before she had acquired sources and contacts as well as experience. As she began to realize just how good she was, she added a generous helping of arrogance to the heavy makeup she plastered on every morning.

Some reporters have an aura about them, an attitude which screams: "My job is the most important in the whole world and I'm better than the lot of you!" Heidi admired people with sharp elbows and soon developed her own. She took up space, even when she was working as a temp. She made demands.

Henning was working for Nettavisen at the time Heidi graduated. He was their crime reporter, but it was also his job to train new reporters and temps, show them the ropes, put them straight and nudge them in the direction of the overall aim: turning them into workhorses who wouldn't need micromanaging in order to deliver top stories that attract Web hits twenty-four/seven.

He enjoyed this aspect of his job. And Nettavisen was a great first job for young journalists, even though most of them had no idea they were driving a Formula 1 car around increasingly congested streets in a media circus that grew bigger every day. Many were unsuited for this life, this way of thinking and working. And the problem was that as soon as he saw the beginnings of a good online reporter, they would leave. They would get offers of new jobs, better jobs, or full-time employment contracts elsewhere.

Heidi left after only four months. She got an offer from *Dagbladet* she couldn't refuse. He didn't blame her. It was *Dagbladet*, after all. More status. More money. Heidi wanted it all and she wanted it now. And she got it.

And she's my new boss, he thinks. Bloody hell. This is bound to end in tears.

"It'll be good to have you back in the saddle, Henning," Kåre enthuses.

Henning says "Mm."

"Morning meeting in ten minutes. You'll be there, won't you?"

Henning says "Mm" again.

"Lovely! Lovely! Got to dash. I've another meeting."

Kåre smiles, gives him a thumbs-up, and leaves. In passing, he slaps someone on the shoulder before disappearing around the corner. Henning shakes his head. Then he sits down on a chair that squeaks and rocks like a boat. A new red notebook, still in its wrapper, lies next to the keyboard. Four pens. He guesses that none of them works. A pile of old printouts. He recognizes them as research for stories he was working on. An ancient mobile telephone takes up an unnecessary amount of space and he notices a box of business cards. *His* business cards.

His eyes stop at a framed photograph resting at an angle on the desk. There are two people in it, a woman and a boy.

Nora and Jonas.

He stares at them without seeing them clearly. Don't smile. Please, don't smile at me.

It'll be all right. Don't be scared. I'll take care of you.

He reaches for the frame, picks it up and puts it down again. Upside down.

The story continues in *Burned*, available in paperback and eBook from ATRIA BOOKS.

COMING SOON FROM MONS KALLENTOFT

Summer Death (June 2013)
Autumn Sonata (March 2014)
Spring Remains (March 2015)

MIDWINTER BLOOD

by Mons Kallentoft

Introducing Malin Fors

Meet Malin Fors. But be careful . . . she's addictive.

Malin Fors. Thirty-four years old. Blonde, athletic. Born, raised, and still residing in the provincial town of Linköping, Sweden. Divorced with a teenage daughter. Single, and always on the verge. Malin is on the verge of being addicted to tequila, and her lover, a journalist named Daniel. She is on the verge of becoming a workaholic, and is always liable to letting her strong emotions and repressed memories dictate her life. On the job, Malin is constantly crossing the border between life and death. She is the most complex superintendent who has ever worked at the Linköping Police, but also the most talented. With intuition, acumen, and courage she steers her colleagues through crime investigations so gruesome they make the darkest of nightmares look like cozy fairy tales. Malin Fors is one of a kind: she is a strong young woman who is trying to find her path in life, a violent and hazardous path, filled with adrenalin and surprises.

Prepare to be chilled by this sample of Scandinavian Mons Kallentoft's *Midwinter Blood,* and witness the dark and grisly reality of police superintendent Malin Fors.

Available as a hardcover and
eBook in June 2012 from
EMILY BESTLER BOOKS

Excerpt from
Midwinter Blood © 2012
by Mons Kallentoft

Sweden

THURSDAY, FEBRUARY 2

L ove and death are neighbors.

Their faces are one and the same. A person need not stop breathing in order to die, and need not breathe in order to be alive.

There are never any guarantees where death or love are concerned.

Two people meet.

Love.

They make love.

And they love and they love and then, after a while, the love runs out, just as abruptly as it first appeared, its capricious source blocked by circumstances, internal or external.

Or else love continues until the end of time. Or else it is impossible from the start, yet still unavoidable.

And is this sort of love, this last sort, is it really nothing but a nuisance?

That's just what it is, thinks Malin Fors as she stands in her dressing gown by the kitchen sink, fresh from the shower, spreading butter on a slice of wholemeal bread with one hand, and lifting a cup of strong coffee to her lips with the other.

Six fifteen, according to the Ikea clock on the whitewashed wall. Outside the window, in the glow of the streetlamps, the air seems to have solidified into ice. The cold embraces the gray stone walls of St. Lars Church, and the white branches of the maples seem to have given up long ago: Not another night of temperatures below minus four; better to kill us outright and let us fall dead to the ground.

Who could love this sort of cold?

A day like this, Malin thinks, is not meant for the living.

Linköping is paralyzed, the city's streets draped limply upon the crust of the earth, the condensation on the windows making the houses blind.

People didn't even make the effort to get to the Cloetta Center last night for the ice hockey, just a couple of thousand instead of the usual full house.

I wonder how Martin's getting on, Malin thinks; her colleague Zeke's son, a local lad, a forward with a chance of a place on the national team and a career as a professional. She can't actually summon up much interest in ice hockey, but if you live in this town it's pretty much impossible to avoid hearing about events on the ice.

Hardly anyone about.

The travel agent's on the corner of St. Larsgatan and Hamngatan mocks with its posters for one exotic destination after the other; the sun, beaches, the unnaturally blue skies belong to another planet, a habitable one. A lone mother is wrestling with a twin buggy outside the Östgöta Bank, the children nestled in black bags, almost invisible, sleepy, obstinate, yet still so unimaginably vulnerable. Their mother slips on patches of ice hidden under a powder of snow, she lurches but drives herself on as though there were no other option.

Winters here are the devil's work.

Malin can hear her father's words within her, his justification a few years ago for the purchase of a three-room bungalow in a retirement village on Tenerife: the Playa de la Arena, just north of Playa de las Américas.

What are you doing right now? Malin thinks.

The coffee warms from within.

You're probably still asleep, and when you wake up it'll be warm and sunny. But here, the frost reigns unchallenged.

Should I wake Tove? Thirteen-year-olds can sleep for ages, right round the clock if they're given the chance, and in a winter like this it would be lovely to hibernate for a few months, not having to go out, and waking up fully restored when the temperature creeps above zero.

Tove can sleep. Let her tall, gangly body rest.

Her first class doesn't start until nine. Malin can see it all in her mind's eye. How her daughter forces herself to get up at half past eight, stumbles to the bathroom, showers, gets dressed. She never wears makeup. And then Malin sees Tove skip breakfast, despite all her cajoling. Maybe I should try a new tactic, Malin thinks: Breakfast is bad for you, Tove. Whatever you do, don't eat breakfast.

Malin drinks the last of the coffee.

The only time Tove ever gets up early is when she wants to finish one of the mass of books she devours almost obsessively; she has unusually advanced taste for her age. Jane Austen. How many Swedish thirteen-year-olds apart from Tove would read something like that? But, on the other hand . . . She's not quite like other thirteen-year-olds, never has to try hard to be top of the class. Maybe it would be good if she did have to make more effort, encounter a bit of real resistance?

Time has run on, and Malin wants to get to work, doesn't want to miss the half hour between quarter to seven and quarter past when she is almost certain to be on her own in Police Headquarters and can plan the day ahead undisturbed.

In the bathroom she takes off the dressing gown. Tosses it on to the yellow synthetic floor.

The glass in the mirror on the wall is a little bowed, and even though it makes her height of five feet seven appear slightly squashed she still looks slim, athletic and powerful, and ready to meet whatever crap comes her way. She's met it before, crap, she's dealt with it, learned from it, and moved on.

Not bad for a thirty-three-year-old, Malin thinks, her self-confidence doing its job: There's nothing I can't deal with, and then the doubt, the old fixed belief, I haven't amounted to much, and won't now, and it's my fault, all my own fault.

Her body. She concentrates on that.

Pats her stomach, takes in a deep breath so that her small breasts stick out, but just as she sees the nipples pointing forward she stops herself.

Instead she quickly bends down and picks up the dressing gown. She dries her blond pageboy with the dryer, letting her hair fall over her prominent but soft cheekbones, forming a pelmet above her straight eyebrows, because she knows that emphasizes her cornflower-blue eyes. Malin pouts her lips, wishes they were bigger, but maybe that would look odd beneath her short, slightly snub nose?

In the bedroom she pulls on a pair of jeans, a white blouse, and a loose-knit black turtleneck sweater.

Glancing at the hall mirror, she adjusts her hair, reassuring herself that the wrinkles around her eyes aren't too visible. She puts on her Caterpillar boots.

Because who knows what lies ahead?

Maybe she'll have to head out into the countryside. The thick, synthetic down jacket she bought from a branch of Stadium at the Tornby shopping center for eight hundred and seventy-five kronor makes her feel like a rheumatic astronaut, her movements sluggish and clumsy.

Have I got everything?

Mobile, purse in her pocket. Pistol. Her constant companion. The gun was hanging on the back of the chair next to the unmade bed. By the mattress with space for two, plus enough room for a decent gap, a gap for sleep and loneliness during the very darkest hours of night. But how can you find someone you can put up with if you can't even put up with yourself?

She has a picture of Janne beside the bed. She usually tells herself that it's there to make Tove happy.

In the photograph Janne is suntanned and his mouth is smiling, but not his gray-green eyes. The sky behind him is clear, and beside him a palm tree is swaying gently in the wind, while in the background you can make out a jungle. Janne is wearing a light blue UN helmet and a camouflage cotton jacket bearing the logo of the Swedish Rescue Services; he looks like he wants to turn round, to make sure that nothing's about to jump out at him from the dense vegetation.

Rwanda.

Kigali.

He's told her about dogs eating people who weren't even dead yet.

Janne went, goes, has always gone as a volunteer. At least that's the official version.

To a jungle so dense that you can't hear the sound of the heart of darkness beating, to mined and blood-drenched mountain roads in the Balkans, trucks with sacks of flour rumbling past mass graves, poorly concealed by sand and scrub.

And it was voluntary from the start, for us.

The short version: A seventeen-year-old and a twenty-year-old meet in a regular old disco in a regular old small town. Two people with no plans, similar but different, yet with some shared essence, ideas that work for both of them. Then, after two years, the event to be avoided at all costs happens. A thin layer of rubber breaks and a child starts to grow.

"We have to get rid of it."

"No, this is what I've always wanted."

Their words slip past each other. Time runs out and their daughter arrives, the sunbeam to end all sunbeams, and they play happy families. A few years pass and a silence falls. Things turn out differently from the way they were planned, if they were planned at all, and each of those involved moves off in his or her own direction, without rhyme or reason.

No explosions, just a damp squib leaving a long trail into history, and even farther into the soul.

The serfdom of love, Malin thinks.

Bittersweet. As she thought back then, after they'd separated, when the removal van was heading for Stockholm and the Police Academy, when Janne moved to Bosnia: If I become really good at getting rid of evil, then goodness will come to me.

Surely it could be as simple as that?

Then love might be possible again. Mightn't it?

On her way out of the apartment Malin feels the pistol pressing against her rib cage. She carefully opens the door to Tove's bedroom. She can make out the walls in the darkness, the rows of books on the shelves, can sense Tove's oddly proportioned teenage body under the turquoise duvet. Tove sleeps almost soundlessly, has done ever since she was two. Before that her sleep was disturbed, she used to wake several times a night, but then it was as if she realized that silence and calm were necessary, at least at night, as if the two-year-old instinctively knew that a person needs to keep the night free for dreams.

Malin leaves the apartment.

Goes down the three flights of stairs to the door of the building. With every step she feels the cold come closer. It's practically below thirty-two in the stairwell.

Please let the car start. It's almost cold enough to freeze the petrol to ice.

She pauses at the door. The chill mist is drifting in waves through the streetlamps' cones of light. She wants to run back upstairs, go into the apartment, tear off her clothes, and creep back into bed. Then it comes again, her longing for Police Headquarters. So: Pull the door open, run to the car, fumble with the key, open the door, throw yourself in, start the engine, and drive off.

The cold takes a stranglehold when she walks out; she imagines she can hear the hairs in her nose crackle with every breath, and feels her tear ducts grow treacly, but she can still read the inscription above one of the side doors of St. Lars: "Blessed are the pure in heart, for they shall see God."

Where's the car? The silver Volvo, a 2004 model, is in its place, opposite the St. Lars Gallery.

Padded, bulky arms.

With difficulty Malin gets her hand into the pocket where she thinks the car keys are. No keys. The next pocket, then the next. Damn. She must have left them upstairs. Then she remembers: They're in the front pocket of her jeans.

Her stiff fingers ache as she thrusts them into the pocket. But the keys are there.

Open now, damn door. The ice has somehow spared the keyhole and soon Malin is sitting in the driver's seat swearing: about the cold, about an engine that merely splutters and refuses to start.

She tries again and again.

But the car refuses.

Malin gets out. Thinks: I have to take the bus, which way does it go?

Damn, it's cold, fucking damn car-fucker, then her mobile rings.

A clawed hand on the angry plastic gadget. She can't be bothered to see who it is.

"Hello, Malin Fors."

"It's Zeke."

"My fucking car won't start."

"Calm down, Malin. Calm down. Just listen. Something big's happened. I'll tell you when I see you. Be with you in ten minutes."

Zeke's words hang in the air. From his tone of voice Malin can hear that something serious has indeed happened, that the coldest winter in living memory just got a few degrees less forgiving, that the cold has just shown its true face.

The story continues in *Midwinter Blood,* available in June 2012 in hardcover and eBook from EMILY BESTLER BOOKS.

ALSO BY JULIE KRAMER

Killing Kate
Silencing Sam
Missing Mark
Stalking Susan

SHUNNING SARAH

by Julie Kramer

Introducing Riley Spartz

TV reporter Riley Spartz is the star investigative journalist of Channel 3 in Minneapolis. Smart, funny, and compulsively entertaining, she cares as much about justice as she does about ratings. Known for her gutsy determination, she'll stop at nothing to solve the mysteries she covers. In the wild, unpredictable world of television news, Riley stands out for her uncanny ability to unravel each mystery she encounters. Nothing can keep this reporter down— although she is constantly a moving target. Riley has been stalked by serial killers and hunted down by individuals with secrets to hide. Danger defines Riley's world, and it does seem to attract quite the audience . . .

Buckle up for a preview of Julie Kramer's next thriller, *Shunning Sarah*, featuring Minneapolis's investigative reporter Riley Spartz.

Available as a hardcover and eBook in August 2012 from
EMILY BESTLER BOOKS

Minnesota

Excerpt from
Shunning Sarah © 2012
by Julie Kramer

The missing face unnerved me. No eyes, nose, or mouth to lend personality to the cloth doll clutched by the little Amish girl.

My own Raggedy Ann exuded charm while this toy sported plain dress, empty facade. Spooky even.

I felt sorry for my playmate, but could express no true condolences because we didn't share the same language. Instead, I set four cups and saucers on a tree stump for a makeshift tea party.

Our fathers were inside the barn arguing about the price of an old crosscut saw. Mine didn't want to sell the saw because my great-grandparents had used it to build the house where we now lived. While the dusty tool hadn't been used in two generations, the saw told a cherished story of family history.

The other man had immediate, practical plans for the device, but the visit ended badly when it became apparent no deal was forthcoming and the saw would remain behind. Though his beard and wide-brimmed hat masked his expression, he walked like an angry man. Untying the horse, he commanded his daughter join him. She hurried over, absently leaving her plaything behind.

As I stood to return the doll, my eyes fell to a basket of crayons on the ground. A good deed came to mind. Round black eyes. A red triangle nose. Smiley mouth with center lip. Had there been more time, I would have added red striped leggings.

I rushed the doll over to the other girl and handed it up to her in the black buggy. The fresh face greeted her like a new friend, but instead of a smile of gratitude, her eyes grew wide with dismay.

I watched the pair ride out of our farm yard, never to return.

The next day, when I walked to the gravel road to check the mail box, something lying in the ditch caught my eye. The head of the doll rested among the weeds; the cloth body nowhere near.

I didn't tell anyone what had happened, not even my parents.

That night, as I tried to sleep, the image haunted me. But somehow by morning, I had pushed the incident from my mind and didn't think about it for twenty-five years.

"What do you smell, Buddy?"

Josh Kueppes, wearing a neon-orange stocking hat and carrying a shotgun, chased after his dog.

"Maybe bear?"

His voice sounded hopeful as he dreamed of returning home with such a trophy. He'd watched the news the night before and seen reports of a black bear sighted in southeastern Minnesota. So while unusual, his goal wasn't impossible. At least, that's what he told himself.

The school bus had dropped off the ten-year-old outside his family's farmhouse. On the kitchen table, he found a note from his mother that she'd been called to work an evening nursing shift. Quickly, he finished his chores of feeding the chickens and bringing in the mail. Her instructions read that he was supposed to bike over to an older friend's place down the road, spend the night, and go to school with him the next morning. Josh smiled at the prospect of fun.

But his mother's absence also presented a sneak opportunity. For a hunt. So he donned his camouflage jacket.

He and Buddy, a tan mixed breed, ran through a lightly snow-covered farm field. The corn had been harvested but the stalks not yet plowed under. An early cold spell hit just as September was turning into October. He stumbled a couple of times before reaching a line of trees growing in a depression in the ground.

His dog bayed, just like a real hunting hound.

Josh's eyes grew wide.

He held the gun steady, finger on the trigger, as he glanced around to see what had attracted the animal's attention. He didn't want to be ambushed, but theirs seemed the only tracks. He looked upward hoping to at least face off with a raccoon in the branches . . . but they were empty.

He didn't have enough experience to realize that broad daylight was less conducive to hunting wildlife than dawn or dusk. Buddy barked some more and Josh noticed a hole in the earth that looked curious. Maybe a bear den. He moved closer, but his eyes kept cautiously scanning back and forth for trouble when the ground beneath him collapsed.

He tumbled downward amid dirt and snow and confusion. Gradually, through a reassuring gap of sunshine, he became aware of his dog still above, sounding an agitated alarm that went unheard.

Around him, he smelled an unpleasant odor and as his eyes adjusted to the blackness he realized he was not alone in the bottom of the pit.

Deep underground, Josh fumbled for his gun. Aimed the weapon toward the sky and pulled the trigger in a calculated call for help.

Nothing happened.

Then he realized the safety was on, and tried again.

Almost immediately, he wished he hadn't.

Instead of escape . . . instead of rescue. . . . the shot sent more dirt downward like an avalanche burying him and a grisly secret.

The woman's eyes freaked Josh. Her eyes were cloudy, her head crooked, and parts of her face had black splotches. She reminded him of a zombie movie he'd seen once at a friend's house. But the creatures in the film were billed as Living Dead and Walking Dead. He had no doubt this woman was dead dead. And would never walk again.

Because she would not or could not shut her eyes, he shut his.

Every time he opened them a crack, she was still there—staring back. The rest of her body remained wrapped in a colorful blanket.

"Buddy!" He called for his dog, but no answer.

Josh hoped his pet had gone for help. He pulled his stocking cap over his face. That act improved the view, but did nothing for the smell. Hours passed and he began to wonder how much time must slip by before he resembled the lifeless women trapped beside him.

His fingernails still hurt from clawing his way free of the dirt. He wished the landslide had buried his companion. Though some of her body had been covered with earth, her head had been spared. Josh thought about kicking soil over her face so he wouldn't have to look at her. But that seemed wrong.

He pushed his hat back so he could see better and after more digging, he found the shotgun. He was afraid to pull the trigger again, but just clutching the weapon was a security blanket.

Josh sensed the sun going down. With nighttime, he wouldn't see the dead woman. But maybe seeing her in her corner was better than imagining her coming at him in the dark. If he weren't so cold, he could be convinced he was in hell.

He decided the corpse didn't need her blanket anymore. And huddling under it might bring him warmth and help him sleep. He was sure he'd feel safer. He stood, grabbed one end of the bedding, and, with a few jerks, tore the cover from her body.

Her face hit the ground, but her body rolled onto its side so she continued staring. And even though the light in the pit was dim, he could tell the woman was naked. Horrified, Josh crawled under the blanket and pulled it over his head.

The house was full of photographs of Josh. School. Sports. Holidays. Some clipped under refrigerator magnets. Others mounted in frames hanging on the entry wall. She even had scrapbooks starring the blond, freckled boy. But she resisted sweet memories and grabbed a current school picture—sticking it in the front door in case the cops got there before she got back.

The dog kept barking and getting in her way while she tried to concentrate on where best to search for her missing son. And suddenly she realized she'd been stupid for nearly an hour.

"Come on, Buddy. Where is he? Where's Josh?"

The dog let out a howl and started running toward the farm fields, eager for her to follow.

"Good boy. Take me to him."

She vowed that if Josh had run off, she would hug and not yell. "Just let him be safe," she prayed. She said safe louder than the other words. Because safe is such a comforting word. And as if saying it with a ring of confidence makes it more likely to be true.

Soon, on the ground, she noticed a trail of footsteps—mostly beast, but definitely some boy prints. She was relieved the dog stuck to the path of tracks in the snow.

The last mark of Josh.

The story continues in *Shunning Sarah*, available in August 2012 in hardcover and eBook from EMILY BESTLER BOOKS.

ALSO BY WILLIAM KENT KRUEGER

Trickster's Point (August 2012)

Vermilion Drift

Heaven's Keep

Red Knife

Thunder Bay

Copper River

Mercy Falls

Blood Hollow

The Devil's Bed

Purgatory Ridge

Boundary Waters

Iron Lake

NORTHWEST ANGLE

by William Kent Krueger

Introducing Cork O'Connor

Cork O'Connor, the former sheriff of Tamarack County, is a man of tremendous resource and mixed heritage. Part Irish American and part Ojibwe, he straddles two cultures that, more often than not, are at extreme—sometimes violent—odds. He's a family man who'd rather toss a football with his son than tote a gun. But he understands only too well that he lives in a place where winter isn't the only thing that can kill the unwary, where wolves share the woods with predators who walk on two legs, and where, in order to protect those he loves, even a good man must be willing to do the unthinkable.

———————

Read on for a look at the first chapter of William Kent Krueger's *Northwest Angle* where you will meet Cork O'Connor.

Currently available as a paperback and eBook from
ATRIA BOOKS

Minnesota

Excerpt from
Northwest Angle © 2011
by William Kent Krueger

Later, when it no longer mattered, they learned that the horror that had come from the sky had a name: derecho.

At the time, all they knew was that the day had begun with deceptive calm. Rose was up early, though not as early as the men, who'd risen at first light and had taken the dinghy across the broad channel to fish. She made coffee and sat on the deck of the houseboat and said her daily prayers while a bright lemon sun rose above the lake and islands. She began with a prayer of thanksgiving for all she had—especially her husband and her family—then, as always, prayed mostly for the people who, in life, despaired. She prayed for those whom she knew personally and for the greater multitude she didn't. At last, she said her amen and gave herself over to the pure pleasure of the still morning.

Anne was up next and then Jenny, and the three women sat in deck chairs on the forward platform, sipping coffee, talking quietly, watching the sun crawl the sky, waiting for the men.

When she heard the dinghy's old outboard cutting through the morning calm, Rose got up and said, "I'll start the potatoes."

Anne stood up, too. "Let me give a hand, Aunt Rose."

"No," she said. "You and Jenny sit. Talk. It's what sisters should do. You almost never see each other these days."

She went to the galley to prepare breakfast. She planned to roast potatoes with onions and red peppers and tomatoes. She thought she would scramble eggs with chives and cream cheese. She would slice melons and strawberries and toss them in a bowl with plenty of fat blueberries. And there would be, she was almost certain, fresh fish to fry.

She heard the men as they pulled alongside and tied up to the houseboat and clambered aboard. She heard Cork say, "Beer and pretzels," and she hoped he wasn't talking about breakfast.

Mal stepped into the galley, smiling hugely, and held up a stringer full of fat yellow perch. "The hunter home from the hill," he said.

"You shot them?" Rose replied. "Not very sporting."

Mal kissed her cheek and started toward the sink.

"Uh-uh," she said. "Those get cleaned on deck." She took him gently and turned him toward the door. "When you have them filleted, bring them in and I'll fry them up."

Stephen came in and went straight to the canister Rose had filled with chocolate chip cookies the day before. He took a handful and said, "Okay, Aunt Rose?"

"Don't spoil your breakfast."

"Are you kidding? I could eat a moose. Can I have some milk, too?"

He left with the cookies and a plastic tumbler filled to the brim. Moments later, Rose heard him talking with his sisters on deck and laughing.

The rented houseboat had a table large enough for all of them to gather around, and they ate amid the clatter of flatware against plates and the lively symphony of good conversation. Anne and Jenny offered to clean up, and they gave Stephen a hard time until he agreed to help. Mal showered, then Cork, and afterward both men settled down to a game of cribbage. The kids finished the dishes, put on their swimsuits, and dove into the lake. Rose set a deck chair in the shade under the forward awning of the houseboat. She sat down to read, but her mind quickly began to wander.

Nearly two years had passed since Jo had been lost in the Wyoming Rockies. Nearly two years dead. And Rose stilled missed her sister. Her deep grieving had ended, but there was a profound sense of something lacking in her life. She had taken to calling this the Great Empty. The kids—"kids" she thought them, though Jenny was twenty-four, Anne twenty-one, and Stephen almost fifteen—splashed and laughed in the water, yet she knew that they felt the Great Empty, too. Cork never talked about his own feelings, and Rose understood that the avoidance itself was probably a sign he was afflicted as well. She wished she knew how to help them all heal fully. In the days when he'd been a priest, Mal had often dealt with death and its aftermath, and he advised her that healing came in its own time and the best you could hope for was to help ease the pain along the way.

"And does everyone heal in the end?" she'd asked her husband.

"Not everyone," he'd said. "At least, not in my experience."

She watched the kids in the water and Cork at the table slapping down his cards, and she breathed in the pine-scented air above that distant, isolated lake, and she prayed, "Let us heal, Lord. Let us all be whole again."

In the early afternoon, Cork said, "It's time, Jenny."

She looked up from the table where she'd been writing, put the pencil in the crease between the pages, closed her notebook, and stood.

"How long will it take?" she asked.

"Less than an hour, if we go directly. But today we're going to make a little side trip."

"Where?"

"You'll see."

Her father liked mysteries, large and small. She understood it was part of what drew him through life, the need to find answers. In a way, it was also what drove her, but they went about it differently. He'd been a cop most of his life and now he was a PI. She, on the other hand, was a writer.

Stephen came from the galley, one hand filled with potato chips. "Can I go?"

"Not this time," his father said. "Jenny and I have things to discuss."

Things to discuss, she thought. *Oh, God.*

"Ah, come on," Stephen said.

Cork shook his head. "Oz has spoken. But if you want to help, go fill the motor on the dinghy with gas."

"I didn't say I wanted to help. I said I wanted to go."

"And now you're going to help," Cork said. He turned to Jenny. "Wear your swimsuit and bring your camera."

"Why?"

"You'll see."

Mysteries, she thought with a silent sigh. But maybe, if they were interesting enough, they would keep her father away from the things he wanted to discuss.

Early September. The air thick on the lake and the sky a weighty blue. The weather, he'd been told, was unusual for that time of year so far north. Hot beyond anyone's memory. Usually by the end of August fall was already solidly in the air. But not this year. The intense heat of the afternoon was bearable only because of the wind generated by the dinghy speeding over smooth water.

Though they were in Canada, Cork knew he could just about throw a stone onto U.S. territory. They were on the Lake of the Woods, a body of water roughly eighty miles long and sixty miles wide, containing over fourteen thousand islands. That's what he'd been told in Kenora, anyway. The lake straddled the U.S.-Canadian border. Border? Cork shook his head, thinking how easily that international marker was crossed on this lake. There was no line on the water to delineate one nation from the other. Kitchimanidoo, the Creator, had made the land a boundless whole. It was human beings who felt the need for arbitrary divisions and drew the lines. Too often, he thought, in human blood.

He held the tiller of the little Evinrude outboard, guiding the dinghy southwesterly across broad, open water toward a gathering of islands humped along the horizon. In the half hour since they'd left the houseboat, he hadn't exchanged a word with Jenny. Which, he strongly suspected, was just fine with her.

The lake was beautiful and, like so many things of beauty, deceptive. The water that day was like glass. The vast size of the lake suggested depth, but Cork knew that beneath the tranquil surface lay reefs and rocks that in the blink of an eye could slit a hull or chew the blades off a prop. He'd been using GPS to follow the main channel between the islands and had been keeping a good speed. But south of Big Narrows he swung the boat west out of the channel, slowed to a crawl, and entered an archipelago composed of dozens of islands, large and small. The shorelines were rocky, the interiors covered with tall pine and sturdy spruce and leafy poplar. Cork eased the boat patiently along, studying the screen of the Garmin GPS mounted to the dash, into which he'd downloaded a program for Lake of the Woods. The water was the color of weak green tea, and he told Jenny, who sat in the bow, to keep her eyes peeled for snags that the GPS couldn't possibly indicate. After fifteen minutes of careful navigation, he guided the dinghy up to the rocky edge of a small island. He eased the bow next to a boulder whose top rose from the water like the head of a bald man, and he cut the engine.

"Grab the bow line and jump ashore," he told Jenny.

She leaped to the boulder, rope in hand.

"Can you tie us off?"

She slid a few feet down the side of the boulder and leaped nimbly to shore, where she tied the boat to a section of rotting fallen timber.

Cork stepped to the bow, leaped to the boulder, then to shore.

"Got your camera?" he asked.

Jenny patted her belt where her Canon hung in a nylon case.

"Okay," Cork said. "Let's take a hike."

The island was nearly bare of vegetation and was dominated by a rock formation that rose conelike at the center. Cork led the way along the rock slope, following the vague suggestion of a trail that gradually spiraled upward around the cone. All around them lay a gathering of islands so thick that no matter which way Cork looked they appeared to form a solid shoreline. Between the islands ran a confusing maze of narrow channels.

"Where are we?" Jenny asked.

"Someplace not many folks know about. Probably the only ones who do are Shinnob."

He used the word that was shorthand for the Anishinaabeg, the First People, who were also known as Ojibwe or Chippewa. Anishinaabe blood ran through Cork and, therefore, through his daughter Jenny.

"On a map, this island doesn't have a name," Cork said. "But Shinnobs call it Neejawnisug."

"What does it mean?"

"I'll tell you in a minute."

They reached the top, which was crowned by a great white stone that looked as if it had been cleaved by an ax. The southern side was rounded and pocked, but the north side was a solid face ten feet tall. It lay in full sunlight, golden, and when Jenny saw that glowing face of rock, her eyes went large.

"Pictographs," she said. "They're beautiful, Dad. Do you know what they mean?"

Cork studied the figures painted in ocher that covered the face of the stone.

"Henry Meloux told me they're a kind of invocation to Kitchimanidoo for safety. He said the Anishinaabeg who drew them were being pursued by Dakota and had come to hide. They left the children here, and that's why they call it Neejawnisug. It means 'the children.' They left the women, too, and went off to fight the enemy. They trusted this place because there are so many islands and so many channels that it's almost impossible to find your way here."

"You found it easily enough."

"When I was sixteen, Henry brought me. *Giigiwishimowin*," Cork said.

"Your vision quest," Jenny interpreted.

"By then it was no longer a common practice among the Ojibwe," Cork said. "But Henry insisted."

"Why here?"

"He never told me."

"Did you receive your vision?"

"I did."

Jenny didn't ask about her father's dream vision, and if she had, he probably wouldn't have told her.

"Have you been here since?"

"Never."

"How did you find it so easily? I mean, after so many years?"

"I spent a long afternoon coming here with Henry. He made me memorize every twist and turn."

"That had to be forty years ago. A long time to remember."

"You mean for an old man."

"I couldn't find my way back here."

"If it was important, I bet you could."

Jenny snapped photos of the drawings on the stone and, for a long time, was silent. "And did Kitchimanidoo hide the children successfully?" she finally asked.

"I don't know. Nor did Henry."

He could see her mind working, and that was one of the reasons he'd brought her. Unanswered questions were part of what drove her. He was uncertain how to broach the other reason he'd asked her to come.

"God, it's hot," Jenny said, looking toward the sun, which baked them. "Not even a breath of wind."

"Dog days."

"Not technically," she said.

"Technically?" He smiled. "So when are dog days? Technically."

"According to the *Farmers' Almanac*, the forty days from July third through August eleventh."

He shook his head. "You're way too precise in your thinking. Your mom, she was the same way."

Jenny brought her gaze to bear on her father. "She was a lawyer. She had to be precise. Legal strictures. I'm a journalist. Lots of the same strictures apply." She looked away, down at the water a hundred feet below. "Mind if I take a dip before we go on?"

"No. Mind if I join you?"

They descended the cone and retraced their path to the boulder where the boat was secured. They'd worn their bathing suits under their other clothing, and they quickly stripped. Jenny slipped into the water first and Cork followed.

The lake had been warming all summer, but even so it still held a chill that was a wonderful relief to the heat of the day.

"So?" Cork said, in clumsy opening.

His daughter turned her head to the sky and closed her eyes and lay on her back, so that her ears were below the surface and she could pretend not to hear him.

"I just want to know one thing. And I know you can hear me."

"It starts with one thing," she said with her eyes still closed. "It ends up everything. That's how you operate."

"Old dog, old trick," he said, waited a moment, then repeated, "So?"

She righted herself, treaded water, and gave in. "All right, what do you want to know?"

"Are you going to marry him?"

"That's a complicated question."

"I think the question is fairly simple."

"Well, I can't answer it."

"Because of you or him?"

"It's a decision we're both involved in."

"You'd tell your mother," he said.

"She wouldn't put me on the rack."

"Have I?"

"You will if you don't get an answer."

"I suppose you've talked to Aunt Rose."

She didn't reply, but her silence itself gave him his answer.

"But you won't talk to me."

"There are things women understand, Dad."

"There are things fathers should be let in on. Look, I don't know why you can't give me a straightforward answer, and that's what concerns me."

"There are issues we need to settle first."

"Children?"

"Ah, children," she said, as if she suddenly understood. "That's why you brought me here to show me those pictographs. This is all about children, isn't it?"

"Not completely. But you indicated there are issues," he said. "And I'm betting that's one. He doesn't want them, does he?"

"Maybe it's me who doesn't."

"Is it?" Again, her silence was his answer. "You've been down this road before, Jenny."

"See? Right there." She lifted her arm and pointed an accusing finger at him. Water dripped from the tip in crystal pearls. "That's why I don't talk to you."

"It was only an observation."

"It was a criticism, and you know it."

"I didn't mean—"

"I'm finished swimming. Let's go."

He'd blown it. In his imagining, the discussion had gone differently, had ended with them understanding each other, touching heart to heart in the way they used to when she was much younger. Instead he watched her breaststroke away from him to the dinghy, leaving him feeling stupid and treading water.

They threaded their way out of the convoluted gathering of islands. Jenny sat rigid in the bow, fiercely giving him her back. As soon as they hit the open water of the main channel, he headed the dinghy again toward the southwest.

When he saw the sky there, he was, for a moment, stunned breathless.

"Dad?" Jenny said from the bow. She'd seen it, too, and she turned back to him, fear huge in her eyes.

"Good God Almighty," he whispered.

The story continues in *Northwest Angle*, available in paperback and eBook from **ATRIA** BOOKS.

LAST WILL

by Liza Marklund

Introducing Annika Bengtzon

Annika Bengtzon is a courageous and compassionate woman, but there is also a dark and sometimes destructive streak within her. Her character evolves distinctly throughout the series: from a married mother of two and victim of abuse to divorced single mother. Annika is an incurable workaholic, completely dependent on the affirmation she receives for being a successful reporter. She has few close relationships, but loves her family deeply. The conflict between her professional ambition and the demands of family is strong for Annika. Ultimately, her authenticity makes her who she is. Stubborn to the point of idiocy, and disastrously bad at cooperation with anyone she doesn't like, Annika often makes bad choices. She is constantly faced with questions of evil and justice, and her ambition to report the truth often places her in life-threatening situations. Annika is constantly exposed to life-threatening violence in her effort to write the ultimate story—but she does it anyway.

Immerse yourself in this gripping scene from Liza Marklund's upcoming mystery, *Last Will*, featuring the daring and ambitious Swedish reporter Annika Bengtzon.

Available as a hardcover
and eBook from
EMILY BESTLER BOOKS

Excerpt from
Last Will © 2012
by Lisa Marklund

Sweden

The woman known as the Kitten felt the weight of the weapon dangling under her right armpit. She tossed the cigarette to the ground, lifted her skirt, and thoroughly crushed the butt with the underside of her high-heeled sandals.

Try to find any DNA on that if you can.

The Nobel festivities had been going on inside the banqueting rooms of the City Hall for three hours and thirty-nine minutes now. The dancing was underway, and she could make out the sound of the music in the chill of the street. The target had left the table down in the Blue Hall and was walking up the flight of steps toward the Golden Hall. The text message she had just received on her cell phone had given her the target's position, as precisely as possible under the circumstances.

She sighed and recognized how irritated she felt, and gave herself a mental slap. This job required concentration. There was no room for existential worrying or thoughts of alternative careers. This was all about basic survival.

She forced herself to focus on the immediate future, on the sequence of events she had memorized by going over it again and again until she was bored stiff by it, certain that the job would be carried out successfully.

So now she set off with light and measured steps, one two three, the salt and gravel rough under the thin soles of her sandals. The temperature had fallen below zero, forming patches of ice on the ground, a detail she had hoped for but hadn't been able to take for granted. The cold made her hunched and pale, and was making her eyes water. If they looked red it would be no bad thing.

The police officers in their uniforms and yellow tunics were positioned where they should be, two on each side of the archway that formed the entrance to the Stockholm City Hall. She calibrated her internal resources.

Time for mark number one: pale and beautiful, frozen and cold, cell phone in her hand. Ta dah, showtime!

She stepped into the archway just as a group of happy revelers rolled up from the other direction. The group's voices jangled in the cold air, their happy laughter echoing. The indirect lighting along the façade of the building threw shadows over their cheerful faces.

She looked down and reached the first police officer at the same time as the raucous men started yelling for a taxi. When the cop made an attempt to talk to her she threw out her arms and pretended to slip. The policeman reacted instinctively, the way men do, and he caught her flailing arm in a gentlemanly fashion. She muttered something embarrassed in incomprehensible English, withdrew her cold hand and glided off toward the main entrance, thirty-three measured steps.

So fucking easy, she thought. This is beneath my dignity.

The flagged courtyard of the City Hall was full of limousines with tinted glass, and she spotted the security guards from the corner of her eye. People were streaming out of the building, breath pluming from their mouths in cones. Straight ahead, beyond the cars and the garden, lay the glittering black waters of Lake Mälaren.

She skipped up to mark number two: the entrance to the Blue Hall. An elderly man was blocking the doorway and she had to stop. The man stood to one side to let out a group of elderly women who were following him, and she had to bite her tongue and stand there shivering in the cold while the old fossils creaked out into the courtyard. One intoxicated gentleman said something impertinent as she slipped into the cloakroom with her cell phone in her hand but she ignored him, just left him in her wake and made it to mark number three.

Annika Bengtzon stood up from table number fifty as her dinner partner, the managing editor of the journal *Science*, held her chair for her. She noticed that her legs were a bit unsteady. Her shawl was on the point of sliding down onto the floor and she clutched it more tightly round her waist. There were so many people, so many swirling colors everywhere. Out of the corner of her eye she saw the permanent secretary of the Swedish Academy hurry past her table. God, he was handsome.

"It's been a pleasure," the editor said, kissing her hand before vanishing into the crowd. Annika smiled politely. Maybe he had been a bit upset when she turned down his invitation to dance.

She fiddled with her shawl and checked the time. She didn't have to get back to the newsroom just yet. Anders Wall, the financier, slid past with his wife, as the head of Swedish Television moved in the opposite direction.

Then she felt someone stop right behind her, and she looked round to see Bosse, the reporter for the other main evening paper.

"How many stars do you give the starter?" he said quietly with his lips far too close to her ear.

"Four skulls and crossbones," Annika said, standing quite still, her bare shoulder against the front of his jacket. "How many points does Princess Madeleine's neckline get?"

"Two melons," Bosse said. "The speech by the guy who got the prize for medicine?"

"Eight sleeping pills . . ."

"May I?"

He bowed dramatically. Annika looked round quickly to make

sure the man from *Science* was nowhere nearby. Then she nodded. She quickly pushed her elegant evening bag inside her larger bag and hoisted it onto her shoulder.

Her grandmother's best shawl was draped over her lower arms, and as Annika's skirt crunched, Bosse took her hand and led her toward the steps leading to the Golden Hall. They sailed between the tables, between the flowers and crystal glasses. Annika had skipped most of the wine, just tasting it so she could report on it (which was frankly an insult to the readers, seeing as she didn't know a thing about wine). Even so, she still felt a bit giddy, a bit too light on her feet. She took Bosse's arm as they started to ascend the staircase, holding up her skirt with her other hand.

"I'm going to trip," she said. "I'll fall on my ass and roll all the way down and knock the legs out from under some important politician."

"No one has ever fallen down these stairs," Bosse said. "When they were building it the architect, Ragnar Östberg, made his wife walk up and down it in an evening gown for a whole week, while he adjusted the steps to make sure you could glide up and down and never fall. The staircase has worked beautifully ever since, but his wife snapped and demanded a divorce."

Annika laughed.

Soon she would have to leave the party and go write it up back in the newsroom. Soon the spell would be broken, soon her flowing long dress would turn into a top from H&M and a polyester skirt with enough static electricity for it to do a passable job as a vacuum cleaner.

"It's completely crazy, really, being part of something like this," she said.

Bosse put his hand on her arm and guided her up the last steps the same way the winner of the chemistry prize had just done with the queen.

They emerged onto the long balcony overlooking the Blue Hall, then had to fight their way through the crowd surrounding a drinks table just outside the doors to the Golden Hall.

"One for the road?" Bosse asked, and she shook her head.

"One dance," she said, "then I have to go."

They stepped into the Golden Hall, the fantastic banqueting hall whose walls were covered with artworks and mosaics made with real gold. The orchestra was playing but Annika couldn't hear the music, it was all just a tapestry of sound. All that mattered was that she was here and Bosse had his arm round her back and she was spinning round and round, the golden mosaics swirling.

The vaulted ceiling, limestone floors: the woman known as the Kitten was inside the building itself. Silk crunched and stretched across full stomachs, cravats rubbed against red necks. She slid unnoticed among the other evening gowns, no need to look around. In recent months she had been on a number of guided tours, in three different languages, through the halls and galleries of the City Hall. She had taken pictures and carefully studied the whole arena, she had been on test runs, even test slips, and she knew the exact length of her stride and where she could catch her breath.

It was a pretty impressive building, she had to admit. The architecture was the best thing about this job.

Twelve steps into the Blue Hall.

She stopped under the six-pointed stars of the pillared walkway and collected herself before entering the dizzying space of the hall, 1,526 slightly asymmetrical square meters, the aftermath of the meal, people crowding onto the marble floor, the light sparkling from thousands of glasses. The royal couple were gone, and the security staff had of course gone with them. She allowed herself a brief moment of contemplation, and realized that she would rather have taken part in the dinner than have to do her job. The theme of the meal had been Nordic winds, which actually sounded rather disgusting, but she liked the way it had all been set out.

Damn, she thought, I really have to come up with some other profession.

Oh well. Mark number four. Turn right, narrow shoulders, a quick glance.

She stepped out from the paired granite pillars and set off toward the staircase, ten steps in her high heels. She could hear the music from the Golden Hall clearly now.

A moment later a man was standing in front of her saying something incomprehensible. She stopped and took a step to the side, and then another. The bastard wasn't letting her through, and she was forced to push her way past him and hurried up the forty-two steps, each one thirteen centimeters high, thirty-nine centimeters across.

Then the long balcony of the Blue Hall, seven doorways into the Golden Hall, seven doorways leading to the great works of art in there, *The Queen of Lake Mälaren* and *Saint Erik*.

She skipped on, pushing her way through, efficient now, warm and quick, past doorway after doorway until she reached the very last one. The music was louder, a key change; it was getting close to the end of the piece, and she walked right out among the crowd of dancing partygoers. Now she really had to keep her focus.

For the first time during the whole of this job she felt the familiar tickling sensation, the crackling rush that sharpened her senses, the swaying sense of satisfaction. The millions of mosaic pieces shimmered in her eyes, cutting into her head; she looked round, the musicians over by the ugly *Queen of Lake Mälaren* on the far side were building up to the crescendo. Her eyes scanned the clothes, the people, she had to locate the target *now*.

And there it was.

Right there, on a direct line from mark number five to mark number six, dancing and jigging about. Ha!

Ninety seconds from now. She fired off a text to her wingman, raised her right arm, opened her evening bag and dropped her cell phone in, then felt for the pistol.

At that moment she was jolted by a laughing figure moving just to the left of her, what the fuck? The floor slid for a moment; she lost her balance and took another unplanned step, feeling her heel sink into something soft and her elbow jab at someone's ribs, then a yelp of pain in her ear.

The sound came so unexpectedly that she looked up and stared into a pair of heavily made-up eyes that were reflecting both annoyance and pain.

Shit! Fuck!

She looked quickly away and took the final steps.

The weapon was heavy and solid in her hand. It felt good, and the concentration that finally, finally filled her made all the sounds around her fade away; she was calm and clear. She raised the bag toward the dancing couple, aiming at the man's leg, the first shot. The sound was scarcely audible, the recoil manageable. The man sank to his knees, leaving the woman unshielded. She raised the bag, aimed at the woman's heart, and fired the second shot.

Her hand let go of the weapon, the ruined bag dangling from its strap once more; she refocused her gaze on the oak door, eight steps to the oak door that symbolized the next mark, one two three four five six (now the screaming started) seven eight, made it, and pulled the door open with no problem. It closed silently behind her, four steps to the service lift, two floors down, and then three steps down the slope to the service entrance.

Her focus started to relax, the wonderful rush started to disintegrate.

Not yet, for fuck's sake, she said angrily to herself. This is the tricky bit.

The cold was paralyzing as she stepped out into the south pillared arcade. Ninety-eight slippery, cold bastard steps toward the water, a hundred-meter dash.

The guards in the courtyard stiffened and in unison raised one hand to their ears, oh shit. She'd expected to get a bit further before they found out what had happened. She pulled the gun from her bag as she let the door of the service entrance close behind her. Three guys were guarding the side facing the water; just as planned, she shot them one by one, intending to render them harmless, not necessarily to kill.

Sorry boys, she thought, nothing personal.

A bullet fired from somewhere behind her hit the granite pillar beside her, chipping off a shard of stone that hit her in the cheek, and the unexpected pain made her flinch. She quickly crouched down, pulled off her shoes, and ran.

Her sense of hearing was coming back and she could make out the roar of the powerful outboard motor.

She left the shadows and turned sharply to the right through the garden, frozen grass crunching beneath her feet, cutting into her like needles. Shots were coming from somewhere behind her and she was flying, darting and flying, with the pistol and shoes in her hands as she tried to hold her skirt up.

The sound of the engine cut off as the boat swung in alongside the City Hall.

Winds of ice cut into her skin as she threw herself down the granite steps.

The waves of Lake Mälaren were hitting the hull and splashing over the sides as she landed awkwardly in the stern of the boat.

The feeling of triumph vanished almost immediately and was

replaced by a restless irritation. She felt her cheek, damn, she was bleeding. As long as it didn't leave a scar. And it was cold as fuck as well.

Only when the tower of the City Hall had disappeared behind them and she was taking off her evening gown did she realize that she had lost one of her shoes.

Detective Inspector Anton Abrahamsson's baby was three months old and had colic. The child had been screaming day and night for eight weeks now and he and his wife were at their wits' end. He was able to go off to work and get a break sometimes, but it was worse for his wife. Anton tried vainly to comfort her over the phone: "It has to stop sometime, darling. Has he burped? Have you tried Minifom?"

The emergency call came through to the communications office of the Security Police just as Anton's wife started to sob with exhaustion.

"I'll be home as soon as I can," Anton Abrahamsson said, hanging up on his despairing spouse and angrily snatching up the emergency call. His reaction could probably be explained by the fact that the call didn't come from either the bodyguard unit or any of their own units, but from the regular police.

Which meant that the regular police force, whose primary duties were to look after the traffic and keep curious bystanders away from crime scenes, had a better grasp on the security situation than the Security Police.

That was Anton Abrahamsson's first conclusion.

The second dawned on him a second later:

Someone's going to end up in serious shit because of this.

The third made the hairs on his arms stand up:

Shit. They're here now.

* * *

I have to call the paper, Annika thought.

She had ended up lying face down on the dance floor, the marble ice-cold against her bare arms. A man was throwing up in front of her, another was standing on her hand. She pulled it away without any sense of pain. A woman was shrieking somewhere to her right, skirts brushed over her head. The orchestra stopped playing in the middle of a note, and in the sonic vacuum the screams echoed like an icy wave around the Blue Hall and out into all the rooms of the City Hall.

Where's my bag? she thought and tried to get up, but was knocked on the head and sank back down.

A moment later the people around her vanished and she was being lifted up out of the crowd of people, a dark-gray suit sitting her down with her back to the rest of the hall. She found herself staring at a dark oak door.

I have to get hold of Jansson, she thought, and tried to look round for her bag. She'd left it by the copper doors leading to the Three Crowns Chamber, but all she could see now was a mass of people milling about and dark-gray men rushing in.

Her knees started to tremble and she felt the familiar rush of angst but managed to hold it at bay, this isn't dangerous, this isn't dangerous. She forced herself to take deep breaths and see the situation for what it was.

There was nothing she could do.

The mosaic figure on the far wall stared at her encouragingly, its snake-hair floating around its face. A fat woman in a black lace dress turned her eyes up and fainted dead away beside her. A young man was shouting so loudly that the veins on his neck were standing out like rubber bands. A drunk old man dropped his beer glass on the floor with a crash.

I wonder where Bosse's got to? she thought.

Her pulse slowed down, the carpet of noise in her head slowly began to fragment, and she could make out words and phrases again. She could hear calls and orders, mostly from the dark-gray suits. They were talking in steel-plated voices into wires that snaked from their ears toward their mouths, then down into inside pockets and trouser linings.

"The service elevator is too small, the gurney won't go in—we'll have to take it out through the ceremonial entrance in the tower."

She could make out the words, but not who was saying them.

"The building's secure, over. Yes, we've separated the witnesses and are in the process of emptying the banqueting halls."

I have to get my bag, she thought.

"I have to get my bag," she said out loud, but no one heard her. "Can I get my bag? I need my cell phone."

She turned round. The mass of people was moving slowly now, like ants before the first frost. A white-clad woman came running in from the Three Crowns Chamber, pushing a gurney in front of her, then a man with another gurney, then several men with stetho-scopes and oxygen masks and drips. Further away in the Golden Hall the Nobel banquet guests stood like a wall, faces white, their mouths black holes. All the screaming had stopped and the silence was deafening. Annika could make out the fragmented sound of quiet talking from the white coats, then the bodies were loaded onto the gurneys, and only then did Annika notice the man, the man who had fallen on the dance floor: he was conscious, moan-ing. The woman was lying completely still.

A moment later they were gone.

The noise rose again with ear-splitting force and Annika took her chance. She slunk past two suits and managed to reach her bag. One of them grabbed hold of her just as she was fishing out her cell phone.

"You're not going anywhere," he said with unnecessary force, and she shook herself free.

She rang Jansson's direct line in the newsroom and got three short bleeps in response.

Network busy.

What the . . . ?

Contacts, press, Jansson, press.

Bleep bleep bleep. Network busy.

Contacts, press, Jansson, press.

Network busy.

Annika looked round, trying to find help. Nobody noticed her.

"Your name?"

A man in jeans was standing in front of her, holding a pad and pen.

"Sorry?" Annika said.

"Criminal Investigation Department, can I have your name? We're trying to figure out exactly what happened. Did you see anything?"

"I don't know," Annika said, looking over at the blood on the marble floor, already dark and congealing.

No angels, she managed to think, thank god the angels are keeping quiet.

She shivered and realized that she had dropped her shawl, her grandmother's best shawl that she had worn back when she was a housekeeper at Harpsund, the prime minister's country estate. It was in a heap on the floor next to the vivid pool of blood.

Dry cleaners, Annika thought. Hope it's okay.

"My name's Annika Bengtzon," she said to the police officer. "I'm covering the Nobel banquet for the *Evening Post*. What happened?"

"Did you hear the shots?"

Shots?

Annika shook her head.

"Did you notice anyone suspicious in connection with the shots?"

"I was dancing," she said, "it was crowded. Someone pushed into me, but nothing suspicious, no . . ."

"Pushed? Who was doing the pushing?"

"A woman, she was trying to get through, and she stood on my foot."

"Okay," the policeman said, writing something in his pad. "Wait here and someone will come and get you for questioning."

"I can't," Annika said. "I've got an article to write. What's your name? Can I quote you?"

The man in jeans stepped closer to her and pressed her up against the wall.

"You're going to wait right here," he said, "until I get back."

"Not on your life," Annika said in a voice that threatened to turn into falsetto.

The police officer groaned and dragged her into the Three Crowns Chamber.

My deadline, Annika thought. How the hell am I going to get out of this?

Editor in chief Anders Schyman had just settled into the sofa in his living room with his wife and an Almodóvar film when the night editor rang.

"There's been shooting at the Nobel banquet," Jansson said. "At least five people have been shot, we don't know if they're alive or dead."

Anders Schyman looked at his wife, as she pressed in vain on the remote to get the right subtitles.

"It's the round button," he said, showing her at the same time as the night editor's words landed in his head.

"Annika Bengtzon and Ulf Olsson from pictures are there," Jansson said. "I haven't been able to contact them, the mobile network's jammed. Too much traffic."

"Tell me again," Schyman said, signaling to his wife to pause the film.

"Too much traffic on the mobile network; one thousand three hundred people trying to make calls from the City Hall at the same time, and it's gone down."

"Who's been shot? At the Nobel banquet?!"

His wife opened her eyes wide and dropped the remote on the floor.

"Some were security guards, but we don't know about the others. The ambulances headed off, sirens blaring, toward Sankt Göran Hospital a few minutes ago."

"Damn!" Schyman said, sitting up straight. "When did this happen?"

He glanced at his watch, 10:57 PM.

"Ten minutes ago, fifteen at most."

"Is anyone dead?" his wife asked, but he hushed her.

"This is mad," he said. "What are the police doing? Have they arrested anyone? Where were the shots fired? Inside the Blue Hall? Where were the king and queen? Haven't they got any fucking security in that building?"

His wife laid a calming hand on his back.

"The police have sealed off the City Hall," Jansson said, "no one can get in or out. They're questioning everyone and will start to let people out in half an hour or so. We've got people on their way to get eyewitness accounts. We don't know if they've arrested anyone, but they're certainly still looking for more people."

"What do things look like in the rest of the city?"

"They've stopped all the trains, and the main roads out are blocked off, but planes are still taking off from Arlanda. There aren't many flights left this evening. We've got people heading for the Central Station, the motorways, pretty much everywhere."

His wife gave him a quick kiss on the cheek, then got up and left the room. Pedro Almodóvar's women disappeared into an indeterminate future, their impending nervous breakdowns on hold.

"Have the police said anything?" Anders Schyman asked. "Terrorism, extremists, any suggestion of a threat?"

"They've announced a press conference, but not until 1:00 AM . . ."

Someone shouted in the background and Jansson disappeared for a moment.

"Well," he said when he came back on the line, "things are pretty hectic here. I need some quick decisions: how many extra pages can we add? Can we hold back some of the ads? And who do you think we should get in to do the lead article?"

The darkness hung heavily outside the editor in chief's living room; he could see his own reflection in the glass and heard his wife running a tap out in the kitchen.

I'm starting to get old, he thought. I'd rather spend the evening with Antonio Banderas and Carmen Maura.

"I'm on my way," the editor in chief said.

Jansson hung up without replying.

His wife was standing by the counter making a cup of tea; she turned around and kissed him when she felt his hands on her shoulders.

"Who's been killed?" she asked.

"Don't know," he whispered.

"Wake me up when you get home," she said.

He nodded, his lips touching the back of her neck.

* * *

The Kitten changed to a higher gear and accelerated cautiously. The little motorbike growled encouragingly, its headlight playing over the graveled tarmac of the path.

This really was too damn easy.

She knew that any sense of superiority wasn't good, it increased the risk of carelessness.

But in this case there were no more difficulties. The rest was just a walk in the park.

The job itself had been presented to her as a challenge, and that was what had interested her. After an initial check she had realized how simple it would be, but that wasn't something she had any intention of revealing to her employer. Negotiations had taken place with the understanding that the job was extremely dangerous and difficult, which had obviously had a decisive effect on the size of her fee.

Ah well, she thought. You wanted it to be spectacular. Okay, hope you like it.

She swung into a narrow bikeway. A branch struck her helmet; it was black as the grave. Stockholm was usually described as a major city, a metropolis with glittering nightlife and a functioning security service, which was a laughable exaggeration. Everything outside the city center itself seemed to consist of scrappy patches of woodland. There was a chance that the couple with the dog had seen her and her wingman head off in different directions on their bikes, but since then she hadn't seen a single person.

A major city, she thought scornfully, as she rode past a deserted campsite.

She rolled her shoulders; she was still freezing. Her thick jacket couldn't really thaw her out, and the boat trip in her evening gown had practically frozen her.

Well, now that wretched silk outfit was at the bottom of the lake together with her bag and eight bricks. The sack was made of netting, so the water would rinse through the material, and any biological evidence would be washed away in a few hours. She still had the gun, as well as the one shoe and the cell phone. She was planning to get rid of those somewhere in the middle of the Baltic.

The thought of the other shoe preyed on her mind.

It had her fingerprints on it, she was sure of that. The shoes had been clean of evidence when she set out on the job, but before that last sprint she had taken it off, held it in her hand.

God knows where she'd dropped it.

There was light ahead of her and she realized she had reached the only inhabited road along the whole of the shore. She forced that damn shoe out of her mind, changed down a gear and turned off the path and up onto the road. Streetlights shone among the tightly packed houses. She let the motorbike roll down the slope, following the shoreline. A few youngsters were hanging about by a jetty; they glanced idly at her, then went on laughing and kicking at the gravel.

She knew that all they saw was a single person of uncertain gender on a small motorbike, wearing dark jeans and a helmet with a visor, no memorable features, nothing to stick in the mind.

The street came to an end and she rolled on into thin forest again, glancing quickly at her watch.

She was slightly behind schedule, only a minute or so, because of the frost. The evening she had timed the journey it had been raining, but the road hadn't been slippery.

She accelerated gently, and a moment later it happened.

The tires lost their grip on the ground and she felt the bike disappear from beneath her. Her left leg took the first blow and snapped like a matchstick just below the knee. Her shoulder hit next and dislocated instantly, then she felt a thud as her head hit the ground, thinking: I haven't got time for this.

When she came to again she was lying facedown on the ground. What the hell had happened?

Pain was pulsing through her whole left side, from her head to her toes. The motorcycle was still growling somewhere behind her, its headlight shining into the trees.

She groaned. Fucking fuck. What was she going to do now?

She pulled off her helmet and lay her cheek against the frozen ground for a few seconds, forcing her brain to clear.

At least the bike was still working: she could feel the vibrations of the engine through the ground. But she was in worse shape. Her leg was broken and her shoulder was buggered. Carefully she flexed the right side of her body.

It seemed okay.

She sat up with her left arm hanging uselessly by her side. The joint was dislocated; she'd seen it happen to other people but had never had it happen to her before. Her leg was excruciatingly painful: she could feel the shaft of the bone pressing against the skin just below her left knee.

She shuffled backward until she felt a narrow tree trunk behind her, and groaned again.

The list of possible options she had to choose from was shrinking pretty damn fast.

Using her right side she dragged herself upright, and with a well-judged motion threw herself forward, letting her shoulder hit the tree trunk.

Holy fucking shit!

The pain as her shoulder popped back in was almost unbearable; she had to cling onto the tree with her healthy arm to stop herself from fainting.

When she had pulled herself together she flexed the fingers of her left hand, gently moved her arm, and realized it was working. But there was nothing she could do about her leg.

She leaned down carefully and caught hold of the helmet. Carefully she hopped over to the motorbike, pulled it upright and, with a great deal of effort, hoisted herself up. She had to bite her lip as she put her left foot on the pedal. The pain brought her out in a sweat as she adjusted her position on the seat.

For a moment she wasn't sure which direction she should be going in. The forest looked the same; she couldn't tell where she had come from.

Shit, shit, shit!

She looked at the time, thirteen minutes behind schedule.

Her wingman would wait for half an hour in the boat out at Torö, then she had given him orders to set off for Ventspils.

Fear hit her like a dagger in the chest.

Would this crappy job up at the bloody North Pole turn out to be her last?

She put the helmet on, dropped the visor and put the bike in gear. She turned and rode in what she hoped was a southerly direction, with her left knee jutting out at an indescribably wrong angle.

The story continues in *Last Will*, available in hardcover and eBook from EMILY BESTLER BOOKS.

ALSO BY WALTER MOSLEY

The Easy Rawlins Mysteries

Blonde Faith

Cinnamon Kiss

Little Scarlet

Six Easy Pieces

Bad Boy Brawly Brown

A Little Yellow Dog

Black Betty

Gone Fishin'

White Butterfly

A Red Death

The Leonid McGill Mysteries

When the Thrill Is Gone

Known to Evil

The Long Fall

Other Fiction

The Last Days of Ptolemy Gray

The Tempest Tales

Diablerie

Killing Johnny Fry

The Man in My Basement

Fear of the Dark

Fortunate Son

The Wave

Fear Itself

Futureland

Fearless Jones

Walkin' the Dog

Blue Light

*Always Outnumbered,
Always Outgunned*

RL's Dream

47

The Right Mistake

Nonfiction

*Twelve Steps Toward
Political Revelation*

This Year You Write Your Novel

*What Next: A Memoir
Toward World Peace*

Life Out of Context

Workin' on the Chain Gang

DEVIL IN A BLUE DRESS

by Walter Mosley

Introducing Easy Rawlins

Ezekiel "Easy" Porterhouse Rawlins is a black hard-boiled detective and World War II veteran living in the Watts neighborhood of Los Angeles. He was born in Louisiana, but spent his late childhood and adolescence living on his own in the Fifth Ward of Houston, Texas. His mother died when he was seven years old, and his father abandoned the family (to avoid reprisals after a violent, racially charged confrontation) prior to her death. In the beginning of Walter Mosley's Easy Rawlins mystery series, Rawlins is an unlicensed private investigator (he acquires a license later) with no background or training in law enforcement. He's a proud man trying to cope with the social injustices of his time, as well as his own personal demons, and he doesn't always do a great job of it.

Read on for the first chapter of Walter Mosley's literary classic *Devil in a Blue Dress* where a careful Easy Rawlins accepts the job of finding Daphne Monet.

Currently available as a paperback and eBook from WASHINGTON SQUARE PRESS

Excerpt from
Devil in a Blue Dress © 1990 by Walter Mosley

California

I DROVE BACK to my house thinking about money and how much I needed to have some.

I loved going home. Maybe it was that I was raised on a sharecropper's farm or that I never owned anything until I bought that house, but I loved my little home. There was an apple tree and an avocado in the front yard, surrounded by thick St. Augustine grass. At the side of the house I had a pomegranate tree that bore more than thirty fruit every season and a banana tree that never produced a thing. There were dahlias and wild roses in beds around the fence and African violets that I kept in a big jar on the front porch.

The house itself was small. Just a living room, a bedroom, and a kitchen. The bathroom didn't even have a shower and the backyard was no larger than a child's rubber pool. But that house meant more to me than any woman I ever knew. I loved her and I was jealous of her and if the bank sent the county marshal to take her from me I might have come at him with a rifle rather than to give her up.

Working for Joppy's friend was the only way I saw to keep my house. But there was something wrong, I could feel it in my fingertips. DeWitt Albright made me uneasy; Joppy's tough words, though they were true, made me uneasy. I kept telling myself to go to bed and forget it.

"Easy," I said, "get a good night's sleep and go out looking for a job tomorrow."

"But this is June twenty-five," a voice said. "Where is the sixty-four dollars coming from on July one?"

"I'll get it," I answered.

"How?"

We went on like that but it was useless from the start. I knew I was going to take Albright's money and do whatever he wanted me to, providing it was legal, because that little house of mine needed me and I wasn't about to let her down.

And there was another thing.

DeWitt Albright made me a little nervous. He was a big man, and powerful by the look of him. You could tell by the way he held his shoulders that he was full of violence. But I was a big man too. And, like most young men, I never liked to admit that I could be dissuaded by fear.

Whether he knew it or not, DeWitt Albright had me caught by my own pride. The more I was afraid of him, I was that much more certain to take the job he offered.

THE ADDRESS Albright had given me was a small, buff-colored building on Alvarado. The buildings around it were taller but not as old or as distinguished. I walked through the black wrought-iron gates into the hall of the Spanish-styled entrance. There was nobody around, not even a directory, just a wall of cream-colored doors with no names on them.

"Excuse me."

The voice made me jump.

"What?" My voice strained and cracked as I turned to see the small man.

"Who are you looking for?"

He was a little white man wearing a suit that was also a uniform.

"I'm looking for, um . . . ah . . . ," I stuttered. I forgot the name. I had to squint so that the room wouldn't start spinning.

It was a habit I developed in Texas when I was a boy. Sometimes, when a white man of authority would catch me off guard, I'd empty my head of everything so I was unable to say anything. "The less you know, the less trouble you find," they used to say. I hated myself for it but I also hated white people, and colored people too, for making me that way.

"Can I help you?" the white man asked. He had curly red hair and a pointed nose. When I still couldn't answer he said, "We only take deliveries between nine and six."

"No, no," I said, trying to remember.

"Yes we do! Now you better leave."

"No, I mean I . . ."

The little man started backing toward a small podium that stood against the wall. I figured that he had a nightstick back there.

"Albright!" I yelled.

"What?" he yelled back.

"Albright! I'm here to see Albright!"

"Albright who?" There was suspicion in his eye, and his hand was behind the podium.

"Mr. Albright. Mr. DeWitt Albright."

"Mr. Albright?"

"Yes, that's him."

"Are you delivering something?" he asked, holding out his scrawny hand.

"No. I have an appointment. I mean, I'm supposed to meet him." I hated that little man.

"You're supposed to meet him? You can't even remember his name."

I took a deep breath and said, very softly, "I am supposed to meet Mr. DeWitt Albright tonight, any time after seven."

"You're supposed to meet him at seven? It's eight-thirty now. He's probably gone."

"He told me *any time* after seven."

He held out his hand to me again. "Did he give you a note saying you're to come in here after hours?"

I shook my head at him. I would have liked to rip the skin from his face like I'd done once to another white boy.

"Well, how am I to know that you aren't just a thief? You can't even remember his name and you want me to take you somewhere in there. Why you could have a partner waiting for me to let you in . . ."

I was disgusted. "Forget it man," I said. "You just tell him, when you see him, that Mr. Rawlins was here. You tell him that the next time he better give me a note because you cain't be lettin' no street niggahs comin' in yo' place wit' no notes!"

I was ready to leave. That little white man had convinced me that I was in the wrong place. I was ready to go back home. I could find my money another way.

"Hold on," he said. "You wait right there and I'll be back in a minute." He sidled through one of the cream-colored doors, shutting it as he went. I heard the lock snap into place a moment later.

After a few minutes he opened the door a crack and waved at me to follow him. He looked from side to side as he let me through the door; looking for my accomplices I suppose.

The doorway led to an open courtyard that was paved with dark red brick and landscaped with three large palm trees that reached out beyond the roof of the three-story building. The inner doorways on the upper two floors were enclosed by trellises that had vines of white and yellow sweetheart roses cascading down. The sky was still light at that time of year but I could see a crescent moon peeking over the inner roof.

The little man opened another door at the other side of the courtyard. It led down an ugly metal staircase into the bowels of the building. We went through a dusty boiler room to an empty corridor that was painted drab green and draped with gray cobwebs.

At the end of the hall there was a door of the same color that was chipped and dusty.

"That's what you want," the little man said.

I said thank you and he walked away from me. I never saw him again. I often think of how so many people have walked into my life for just a few minutes and kicked up some dust, then they're gone away. My father was like that; my mother wasn't much better.

I knocked on the ugly door. I expected to see Albright, but instead the door opened into a small room that held two strange-looking men.

The man who held the door was tall and slight with curly brown hair, dark skin like an India Indian, and brown eyes so light they were almost golden. His friend, who stood against a door at the far wall, was short and looked a little like he was Chinese around the eyes, but when I looked at him again I wasn't so sure of his race.

The dark man smiled and put out his hand. I thought he wanted to shake but then he started slapping my side.

"Hey, man! What's wrong with you?" I said, pushing him away. The maybe-Chinese man slipped a hand in his pocket.

"Mr. Rawlins," the dark man said in an accent I didn't know. He was still smiling. "Put your hands up a little from your sides, please. I'm just checking." The smile widened into a grin.

"You could just keep your hands to yourself, man. I don't let nobody feel on me like that."

The little man pulled something, I couldn't tell what, halfway out of his pocket. Then he took a step toward us. The grinner tried to put his hand against my chest but I grabbed him by the wrist.

The dark man's eyes glittered, he smiled at me for a moment, and then said to his partner, "Don't worry, Manny. He's okay."

"You sure, Shariff?"

"Yeah. He's just a little shaky." Shariff's teeth glinted between his dusky lips. I still had his wrist.

Shariff said, "Let him know, Manny."

Manny put his hand back in his pocket and then took it out again to knock on the door behind.

DeWitt Albright opened the door after a minute.

"Easy," he smiled.

"He doesn't want us to touch him," Shariff said as I let him go.

"Leave it," Albright answered. "I just wanted to make sure he was solo."

"You're the boss." Shariff sounded very sure of himself; even a little arrogant.

"You and Manny can go now." Albright smiled. "Easy and I have some business to talk over."

MR. ALBRIGHT went behind a big blond desk and put his bone shoes up next to a half-full bottle of Wild Turkey. There was a paper calendar hanging on the wall behind him with a picture of a basket of blackberries as a design. There was nothing else on the wall. The floor was bare too: plain yellow linoleum with flecks of color scattered through it.

"Have a seat, Mr. Rawlins," Mr. Albright said, gesturing to the chair in front of his desk. He was bare-headed and his coat was nowhere in sight. There was a white leather shoulder holster under his left arm. The muzzle of the pistol almost reached his belt.

"Nice friends you got," I said as I studied his piece.

"They're like you, Easy. Whenever I need a little manpower I give them a call. There's a whole army of men who'll do specialized work for the right price."

"The little guy Chinese?"

Albright shrugged. "No one knows. He was raised in an orphanage, in Jersey City. Drink?"

"Sure."

"One of the benefits of working for yourself. Always have a bottle on the table. Everybody else, even the presidents of these big companies, got the booze in the bottom drawer, but I keep it right out in plain sight. You want to drink it? That's fine with me. You don't like it? Door's right there behind you." While he talked he poured two shots into glasses that he had taken from a desk drawer.

The gun interested me. The butt and the barrel were black; the only part of DeWitt's attire that wasn't white.

As I leaned over to take the glass from his hand he asked, "So, you want the job, Easy?"

"Well, that depends on what kind of job you had in mind?"

"I'm looking for somebody, for a friend," he said. He pulled a photograph from his shirt pocket and put it down on the desk. It was a picture of the head and shoulders of a pretty young white woman. The picture had been black-and-white originally but it was touched up for color like the photos of jazz singers that they put out in front of nightclubs. She had light hair coming down over her bare shoulders and high cheekbones and eyes that might have been blue if the artist got it right. After staring at her for a full minute I decided that she'd be worth looking for if you could get her to smile at you that way.

"Daphne Monet," Mr. Albright said. "Not bad to look at but she's hell to find."

"I still don't see what it's got to do with me," I said. "I ain't never laid eyes on her."

"That's a shame, Easy." He was smiling at me. "But I think you might be able to help me anyway."

"I can't see how. Woman like this don't hardly know my number. What you should do is call the police."

"I never call a soul who isn't a friend, or at least a friend of a friend. I don't know any cops, and neither do my friends."

"Well then get a—"

"You see, Easy," he cut me off, "Daphne has a predilection for the company of Negroes. She likes jazz and pigs' feet and dark meat, if you know what I mean."

I knew but I didn't like to hear it. "So you think she might be down around Watts?"

"Not a doubt in my mind. But, you see, I can't go in those places looking for her because I'm not the right persuasion. Joppy knows me well enough to tell me what he knows but I've already asked him and all he could do was to give me your name."

"So what do you want with her?"

"I have a friend who wants to apologize, Easy. He has a short temper and that's why she left."

"And he wants her back?"

Mr. Albright smiled.

"I don't know if I can help you, Mr. Albright. Like Joppy said, I lost a job a couple of days ago and I have to get another one before the note comes due."

"Hundred dollars for a week's work, Mr. Rawlins, and I pay in advance. You find her tomorrow and you keep what's in your pocket."

"I don't know, Mr. Albright. I mean, how do I know what I'm getting mixed up in? What are you—"

He raised a powerful finger to his lips, then he said, "Easy, walk out your door in the morning and you're mixed up in something. The only thing you can really worry about is if you get mixed up to the top or not."

"I don't want to get mixed up with the law is what I mean."

"That's why I want you to work for me. I don't like the police myself. Shit! The police enforce the law and you know what the law is, don't you?"

I had my own ideas on the subject but I kept them to myself.

"The law," he continued, "is made by the rich people so that the poor people can't get ahead. You don't want to get mixed up with the law and neither do I."

He lifted the shot glass and inspected it as if he were checking for fleas, then he put the glass on the desk and placed his hands, palms down, around it.

"I'm just asking you to find a girl," he said. "And to tell me where she is. That's all. You just find out where she is and whisper it in my ear. That's all. You find her and I'll give you a bonus mortgage payment and my friend will find you a job; maybe he can even get you back into Champion."

"Who is it wants to find the girl?"

"No names, Easy, it's better that way."

"It's just that I'd hate to find her and then have some cop come up to me with some shit like I was the last one seen around her— before she disappeared."

The white man laughed and shook his head as if I had told a good joke.

"Things happen every day, Easy," he said. "Things happen every day. You're an educated man, aren't you?"

"Why, yes."

"So you read the paper. You read it today?"

"Yes."

"Three murders! Three! Last night alone. Things happen every day. People with everything to live for, maybe they even got a little money in the bank. They probably had it all planned out what they'd be doing this weekend, but that didn't stop them from dying. Those plans didn't save them when the time came. People got everything to live for and they get a little careless. They forget that the only thing you have to be sure of is that nothing bad comes to you."

The way he smiled when he sat back in his chair reminded me of Mouse again. I thought of how Mouse was always smiling, especially when misfortune happened to someone else.

"You just find the girl and tell me, that's all. I'm not going to hurt her and neither is my friend. You don't have a thing to worry about."

He took a white secretary-type wallet from a desk drawer and produced a stack of bills. He counted out ten of them, licking his square thumb for every other one, and placed them in a neat stack next to the whiskey.

"One hundred dollars," he said.

I couldn't see why it shouldn't be my one hundred dollars.

WHEN I was a poor man, and landless, all I worried about was a place for the night and food to eat; you really didn't need much for that. A friend would always stand me a meal, and there were plenty of women who would have let me sleep with them. But when I got that mortgage I found that I needed more than just friendship. Mr. Albright wasn't a friend but he had what I needed.

He was a fine host too. His liquor was good and he was pleasant enough. He told me a few stories, the kind of tales that we called "lies" back home in Texas.

One story he told was about when he was a lawyer in Georgia.

"I was defending a shit-kicker who was charged with burning down a banker's house," DeWitt told me as he stared out toward the wall behind my head. "Banker had foreclosed on the boy the minute the note was due. You know he didn't even give him any chance to make extra arrangements. And that boy was just as guilty as that banker was."

"You get him off?" I asked.

DeWitt smiled at me. "Yeah. That prosecutor had a good case on Leon, that's the shit-kicker. Yeah, the honorable Randolph Corey had solid proof that my client did the arson. But I went down on Randy's house and I sat at his table and pulled out this here pistol. All I did was talk about the weather we'd been having, and while I did that I cleaned my gun."

"Getting your client off meant that much to you?"

"Shit. Leon was trash. But Randy had been riding pretty high for a couple'a years and I had it in mind that it was time for him to lose a case." Albright straightened his shoulders. "You have to have a sense of balance when it comes to the law, Easy. Everything has to come out just right."

After a few drinks I started talking about the war. Plain old man-talk, about half of it true and the rest just for laughs. More than an hour went by before he asked me, "You ever kill a man with your hands, Easy?"

"What?"

"You ever kill a man, hand-to-hand?"

"Why?"

"No reason really. It's just that I know you've seen some action."

"Some."

"You ever kill somebody up close? I mean so close that you could see it when his eyes went out of focus and he let go? When you kill a man it's the shit and piss that's worst. You boys did that in the war and I bet it was bad. I bet you couldn't dream about your mother anymore, or anything nice. But you lived with it because you knew that it was the war that forced you to do it."

His pale blue eyes reminded me of the wide-eyed corpses of German soldiers that I once saw stacked up on a road to Berlin.

"But the only thing that you have to remember, Easy," he said as he picked up the money to hand me across the table, "is that some of us can kill with no more trouble than drinking a glass of bourbon." He downed the shot and smiled.

Then he said, "Joppy tells me that you used to frequent an illegal club down on Eighty-ninth and Central. Somebody saw Daphne at that very same bar not long ago. I don't know what they call it but they have the big names in there on weekends and the man who runs it is called John. You could start tonight."

The way his dead eyes shined on me I knew our party was over. I couldn't think of anything to say so I nodded, put his money in my pocket, and moved to leave.

I turned back at the door to salute him good-bye but DeWitt Albright had filled his glass and shifted his gaze to the far wall. He was staring into someplace far from that dirty basement.

———————

The story continues in *Devil in a Blue Dress*, available in paperback and eBook from WASHINGTON SQUARE PRESS.

BLESSED ARE THE DEAD

by Malla Nunn

Introducing Emmanuel Cooper

Emmanuel Cooper is an Englishman who serves as a police officer in 1950s apartheid South Africa. Forced to resign from his position as detective sergeant and be re-classified as "mixed-race" after an incident involving a black woman, Cooper faces many challenges in his work in the racially segregated nation. But Cooper is crafty, tough, resilient, and never backs down from a challenge. He isn't interested in political expediency and has never been one for making friends. He may be modest, but he radiates intelligence and certainly won't be getting on his knees before those in power. As defiant as he is stubborn, Cooper always follows his intuition and never lets anything stand in his way—even it if it's the law. Detective Emmanuel Cooper is a man caught up in a time and place where racial tensions and the raw hunger for power make life very dangerous indeed.

Read on for the first chapter of Malla Nunn's *Blessed Are the Dead*, and meet the brilliant and tortured South African detective Emmanuel Cooper.

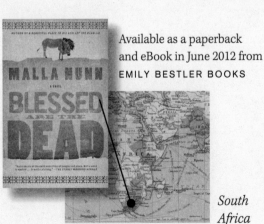

Excerpt from *Blessed Are the Dead* © 2012 by Malla Nunn

Available as a paperback and eBook in June 2012 from EMILY BESTLER BOOKS

South Africa

A ZULU HERD BOY walked quickly up the dirt path, his bony frame bent to meet the steep rise of the mountain. The rhythmic pounding of his bare feet on the rough ground kicked stones loose and raised red dust into the air.

"Higher, ma' baas." The boy was apologetic, afraid of taxing the white policeman in the neat blue suit and the black hat pulled low on his head to block out the light. "We must go higher."

"I'm right behind you," Emmanuel said. "Keep going."

The steady pace was nothing compared to army boot camp or the three years spent in combat, marching between battlefields in Europe during the war. Detective Constable Samuel Shabalala from the Native Detective Branch followed directly behind him and the close rhythm of his breath spurred Emmanuel to keep moving.

"Soon, ma' baas," the boy promised. "Soon."

"I'm still with you," Emmanuel said. The dead were patient. To them, eternity was flexible and time meant nothing. For police detectives, however, time was everything. The sooner the crime scene was located and sketched in detail, the better chance there was of catching the killer.

The herd boy stopped abruptly and then slipped into the lush grass along the edge of the path.

"There, ma' baas." He pointed a skinny finger to the rise. The path snaked behind a sandstone boulder embedded in the grass. "You must go past the rock and up again."

The boy wanted no part of what lay beyond.

"My thanks," Emmanuel said, and turned to look behind him. He saw the path they had traveled from the floor of the Kamberg Valley and the mountains rising in the distance on the other side. Clouds piled on top of each other behind the peaks. The bronze tops of the mountains, some of them dusted with snow, looked like fortresses for gods. There was nothing like the Drakensberg Mountains anywhere else on earth.

"Where to, Sergeant?" Shabalala asked when he drew even with Emmanuel.

"Around that bend," Emmanuel said. "Our guide has dropped out."

They moved on, slowly skirting the boulder. Three Zulu men dressed in traditional cowhides worn over printed cloth stood shoulder to shoulder across the narrow path to form a roadblock. They held hardwood clubs and assegais, hunting spears with rawhide bindings and sharp blades. Together they made an impi, a fighting unit. The tallest of the men stood in the center.

"Suggestions?" Emmanuel asked Shabalala.

The Zulu men gave no indication that they might move from the middle of the path. Military defeat at the hands of the British army and Boer commandos had not cowed them. They stood as their ancestors must have a hundred years ago: fearless masters of their own land.

"Should we wait for the local police?" Shabalala asked. Far below and across the emerald stretch of the valley lay the town of Roselet, the closest source of law enforcement backup.

"The station commander might not get the message for hours," Emmanuel said, referring to the handwritten note he'd stuck to the door of the locked police station an hour ago. A small sandstone bungalow adjacent to the station had also been empty. "I don't want to lose any more time."

"Then we must go together. Slowly. Hands open, like this." Shabalala lifted both hands and showed empty palms to the Zulu men. The gesture was simple, universal. It said, *No weapons. No harm intended.*

Emmanuel did the same.

"Now we must wait," Shabalala said. "Do not look away from them, Sergeant."

Sunshine glinted off the fighters' sharpened spearheads. The weapons were not dusty antiques from a grandfather's hut. The men themselves were no relics, either. It was hard to gauge their age, but they were tall and muscular. Emmanuel figured a lifetime of running up these mountains and hunting game had kept them lethal.

"Never crossed my mind," he said.

"Who are you?" the man in the middle demanded in Zulu. He was the eldest of the three.

"*Sawubona, inkosi*. I am Detective Constable Samuel Shabalala from the Native Detective Branch. This is Detective Sergeant Cooper, the boss of detectives in Durban."

"*Yebo, sawubona*." Emmanuel made the traditional greeting. He let the instant promotion to top boss pass. If Shabalala thought they needed extra status to move ahead, they probably did.

"Cooper. Shabalala. We see you." The elder nodded a greeting but did not smile. "Come. The firstborn child of my father's sister is waiting."

Emmanuel didn't try to work out the connection. Zulus did not have family trees, they had family webs. The men turned and jogged up the slope in formation, weapons held in relaxed hands that were used to the weight.

"You lead," Emmanuel said to Shabalala. The Zulu detective wore the standard Detective Branch uniform, a suit with polished leather shoes and a black fedora hat, but the hills and untamed veldt had been his childhood playground. He knew this land and its people.

They pushed up the steep gradient for two more minutes. An eerie low-pitched moaning swelled and rolled over the treetops before dropping away again in a wave.

"What's that?" Emmanuel asked but didn't slacken his pace.

"The women." The words were spare, stripped down but full of sorrow just the same. Shabalala had heard this sound before.

The Zulus stopped and pointed their assegais to a rock fig growing out almost horizontally from a craggy ledge. The sound was distinct now: female voices crying out and wailing in the bushes.

"They are waiting," the elder Zulu said.

Emmanuel again let Shabalala take the lead. The tall grass and bush thinned out a few yards off the path and a group of women became visible. They sat in a circle, swaying back and forth. The rock fig branched over them like a sentinel. Emmanuel hesitated. One step closer and the sorrow would engulf him and drag him back to a time and place in his own life he'd rather forget.

"Sergeant," Shabalala prompted softly, and Emmanuel walked on. He'd chosen this life among the wounded and the dead. Dealing with the living was a necessary part of the job

"She is here, inkosi." One of the women shuffled to the side to make a gap in the circle through which Emmanuel could approach the body. A black girl lay on the sweet spring grass, gazing up at the soft blue sky and the shapes of darting birds in the air. Her head rested on a rolled-up tartan blanket and tiny red and yellow wildflowers were scattered over the ground. Three or four flowers had fallen into her mouth, which was slightly open.

"We need to get closer," Emmanuel said to Shabalala, and the Zulu detective relayed the request in a low voice. The women broke the circle but gathered again under the branches of a paperbark thorn tree nearby. Their wails subsided and were replaced by the muted sound of swallowed tears.

"Hibo . . ." Shabalala whispered when they were crouched either side of the girl. This was not the messy knifing or domestic argument gone too far they'd been expecting when Colonel van Niekerk personally tapped them on the shoulder for this case.

"Yeah, I know." Emmanuel examined the victim. She was young, maybe seventeen years old, and beautiful. High cheekbones, gracefully arched brows and full lips were features that would have kept into old age. No more. All that was left was a glimpse of what might have been.

"No signs of a struggle," he said. The girl's fingernails were neatly shaped and unbroken. The skin on her wrists, neck and upper arms was unmarked. "If her eyes were closed I'd say she was sleeping."

"Yes," Shabalala agreed. "But she did not walk here. Someone brought her to this place. Look at her feet, Sergeant."

Emmanuel bent lower to get a better view. Dirt and broken grass stalks were stuck to the rough-skinned heels and slim ankles. "She was dragged here and then laid down."

"I think so," Shabalala said.

Under normal circumstances, with a wooden barricade in place and a few uniformed police on guard, Emmanuel would have pushed aside the neckline of the girl's dress and checked for bruising on the shoulders and under the armpits. Modesty was never a concern of the dead. The presence of the gathered Zulu women stayed his hand and he pulled a notebook and pen from his jacket pocket.

To Shabalala he said, "She wasn't dumped or hidden under branches."

He wrote the letters *R.I.P.* on the first page. Rest in peace. Whoever had dragged the victim to this spot had wanted her to rest in a peaceful place with a rock fig above and a wide valley below.

"And the flowers." Shabalala stood up and surveyed the hillside. Clumps of bright red and yellow broke the stretch of green. "They are growing all around but I do not think the wind blew them to this place."

"It looks like they were deliberately scattered over her," Emmanuel said, picking up a tiny red bloom from the crook of the girl's elbow. He understood this need to mark the fallen. Small gestures made the difference even in the white heat of war: a helmet placed on the chest or a poncho thrown over the face of a dead soldier, the closest thing available to a eulogy or a farewell.

Emmanuel scribbled *loved* on the next clean page. First time that word had come up at a crime scene. There was no doubt the girl had been loved and was loved still. Even now, in death, a circle of grieving women and a group of armed men guarded her.

"How long do you think she's been here?" he asked Shabalala. It couldn't have been more than twelve hours, he imagined. The vultures and wildcats hadn't begun to disassemble her body.

"One day and a half." Shabalala walked the perimeter of the crime scene, examining snapped twigs and flattened grass. "The women's tracks are from this morning but the deep lines from the girl's heels are from before."

Emmanuel stood up and moved to where Shabalala was bent over a crushed leaf. "You sure she's been out in the open all that time?"

"*Yebo*, Sergeant. It is so."

"But she's nearly perfect." He glanced at the girl. Her slender legs were a shoulder width apart, the left knee slightly crooked as if she might sit up at any moment and wave hello. The hem of her white calico dress fluttered against her upper thighs—whether blown by the wind or hitched up by a human hand, it was impossible to tell. A pea-sized mark marred the smooth inner surface of her left inner thigh. "No animals have disturbed the body. And there are no signs of injury besides that bruise."

"I see this also," Shabalala said, and paused, reluctant to continue. Other detectives burned oxygen throwing out half-formed theories and detailed explanations of the how and the why of a murder, but not Shabalala. He did not speak unless he was sure of the facts. It was a learned caution. Black detectives rarely added spontaneous comments or joined in the competitive banter that buzzed around a dead body. They were junior partners, brought onto a case only if special knowledge of "native situations" was needed.

"Tell me," Emmanuel said. "It doesn't have to make sense."

Bullshit theories spun out of thin air had their uses.

"What I see is strange," Shabalala said.

"Tell me anyway."

The Zulu policeman pointed to scuff marks in the dirt and to a heavy stick lying on the grass. "I think that the animals did not come near because the one who brought the girl to this place kept them away."

"You have to explain," Emmanuel said. The indentations in the dirt meant nothing to him and the stick was clean of blood or other signs of use.

"A man . . ." the Zulu detective hesitated and moved to the right to examine another patch of disturbed earth. "A small man was here. He ran from where the girl is lying to here with the stick. See this, Sergeant?"

The spoor of a wildcat was identifiable even to Emmanuel's untrained eye. "He moved out to defend the body from predators. That means he must have stayed with her."

" *Yebo*. I believe this."

Emmanuel underlined the word *loved* and then added *protected*.

"Was he a human predator and the girl his prey?" he wondered aloud. People often killed the one they loved the most.

Shabalala shook his head, frustrated at not having the full picture. "I cannot say if this man was the one to harm her. People have come to this place and walked all around. Some of the women scooped the earth with their hands and threw their bodies in the dirt. Many tracks have been lost. A man brought her here and kept the animals away. That is all I see."

"We know a lot more than when we got here," Emmanuel said.

"Let's take another look at the body and then we'll talk to the women, see what they can tell us about the victim."

"*Yebo,*" Shabalala agreed, and they walked back to where the girl lay. A yellow grasshopper had landed on the curve of her neck and was busy cleaning its wings and long antennae.

"No visible injuries," Emmanuel said, and waved the grasshopper away. Natural causes couldn't be ruled out yet. "We'll have to turn her over, find what's hidden."

They rolled the body onto its side so the back was visible. A soft gasp came from the women under the paperbark thorn. The girl was theirs and still alive in their minds. To see how easily she slipped from their embrace and into the hands of strangers shocked them.

"There," Emmanuel said. A small hole, the size of a thumbtack head, punctured the white calico dress just above the waist. Spots of blood speckled the fabric. "Could be a bullet entry wound."

"Maybe a knife also." Shabalala pressed his fingertips into the ground where the girl had been lying and checked them. "The soil and grass are damp with blood but not soaked."

"She didn't bleed to death. But this isn't a good time to look at the entry wound." The mourners had edged closer to the crime scene and their anxiety was palpable. "The district surgeon will have answers for us in a few days. Till then we can only guess at what made the wound. Lay her on her back and let's find out who she is."

They rolled the girl's body into its original position and Shabalala pushed the tartan blanket under her head again, as if she might be uncomfortable without the support.

"Do you want to take the questioning?" Emmanuel asked. He spoke Zulu himself, had mixed in with Zulu boys and girls and even been in and out of their homes till the violent events of his adolescence had seen him and his sister banished to a remote cattle farm and then to a whites-only boarding school. This situation was different.

"You must start," Shabalalala said. "They will know that the police are serious if a white policeman is in charge."

That made sense. Native policemen and detectives were armed with sticks and given bicycles to ride. They were not allowed to drive police vehicles. The power of the gun and the car and the law itself was in the hands of Europeans. Shabalala knew that. The rural women waiting under the tree knew it also.

"Speak in Zulu," Shabalala suggested in a quiet voice. "And thank them for looking after the girl until we came."

"Will do," Emmanuel said. "If my Zulu isn't up to scratch you'll have to take over."

He approached the mourners. There were six of them, barefoot and dressed in heavy black skirts that fell below the knee. Supple cowhide aprons covered their breasts and each wore a fine black head covering decorated with porcupine quills to signify they were married women: mothers of the clan.

"I'm sorry for your loss," Emmanuel said in Zulu, addressing a woman at the front of the group who was being held up by her elbows to stop her from collapsing onto the ground. She possessed the same beauty as the girl lying on the grass. Surely the victim's mother or aunt. "Thank you for keeping her safe until we came. We are grateful."

"Amahle Matebula," the woman said. "That is my daughter's name."

Amahle meant "the beautiful one." Emmanuel had run the streets of Sophiatown with a fat Zulu girl of the same name. She was meaner and tougher than most of the street boys and proud of it. Shoplifting was her speciality; she sold the goods for a small profit and a kiss from the boys she favored. He'd used her services sparingly, buying last-minute Christmas gifts from her stolen haul.

"You named your daughter well." Emmanuel introduced himself and Shabalala before retrieving his notebook and pen. "What may I call you?"

"Nomusa."

Mother of grace. Another perfect name. Emmanuel was certain his birth mother had named him. He was certain also that she must have been in one of those bright, dazzling moods that overtook her every few months, when she shone like a fire.

"Tell me about Amahle," Emmanuel said. "When did you last see her?"

"Friday morning. It was still dark outside. She went to work but did not come home." Nomusa's weight sagged and the women holding her upright couldn't take the strain. They eased her to the ground and propped her up with their hands and shoulders. Emmanuel and Shabalala crouched and waited for the women to settle.

"Where did she work?" Emmanuel asked when Nomusa lifted her head off her chest. Five more minutes and she would not even be able to do that.

"At the farmhouse of Inkosi Reed." A gray-haired woman to Nomusa's right whispered in her ear and she added, "Little Flint Farm. It is close to here. In the valley."

"What time did Amahle normally leave work?" Other girls, more fortunate ones, would be home from school in the early afternoon, filling exercise books with the vocabulary words of the day.

"Sundown. Amahle knew the paths over the mountains and she never tarried." Nomusa lifted her head high now, spurred on by a sudden flash of anger. "This was told to the white policeman on Saturday morning but he did not come! He did not look for her!"

"You reported her missing to the commander at the Roselet Police Station?" Emmanuel asked.

"*Yebo*. Constable Bagley. That very man," Nomusa said. "He did not care to find my daughter and now the ancestors have taken her."

"Easy, my sister." One of the women placed a hand on Nomusa's shoulder. No good came from criticizing the police.

"What I say is true." Nomusa shrugged off the hand and leaned in closer to Emmanuel. Rage lit her dark eyes. "The white policeman is a liar. He promised to help but sat on his hands. He cares for no one else's daughters but his own."

"Please, sister," another woman said. "What's done is done."

The finality of the woman's words seemed to drain the anger from Nomusa. Her expression softened and she said to Emmanuel, "From the day my daughter was born her eyes were on the horizon and what was beyond it. I should have kept her by my side but she did not like to be watched over. Now she is gone . . ."

Nomusa covered her face with her hands and began to cry. A woman held her and rocked her like a child as she sobbed. Emmanuel put the notebook away and stood up. Pressing for more information would gain him nothing. Nomusa had become unreachable in her grief.

"Find out who discovered the body and see if the women can help us with a list of people to talk to," Emmanuel said to Shabalala. "I'll search the area for a possible murder weapon."

"Yes, Sergeant." Shabalala shuffled closer to the women and waited patiently for the right moment to speak.

Emmanuel walked away. Grief and despair were part of the job. He was used to it. But there were times, like this one, when the ghosts of the dead from his past tried to break through into daylight instead of waiting for night to fall.

He combed the grass, searching for a knife, a spent bullet casing or a sharpened stick—anything that might have caused the injury to Amahle's back. He could do nothing for the war dead. This death on a Natal hillside, however, he could do something about.

The story continues in *Blessed Are the Dead,* available in June 2012 in paperback and eBook from EMILY BESTLER BOOKS.

COMING SOON FROM KRISTINA OHLSSON

Daisy (February 2013)

UNWANTED

by Kristina Ohlsson

Introducing Fredrika Bergman

Fredrika Bergman has been hired by the Swedish police force as part of a new approach to solving crime: recruiting academic criminologists and psychologists and integrating them into the organization. Fredrika has reluctantly accepted the position with the force simply to advance her career. She is an intellectual and fiercely independent young woman. She has only ever let one man into her heart and that's her former professor: a married man fifteen years her senior with whom she has been having a ten-year affair. Fredrika carries around a lot of anger. The anger stems not only from her futile love, but her broken dreams of becoming a musician and her pig-headed colleagues, the "real" policemen who are highly suspicious of her role and have little tolerance for her ideas and input. A true academic, Fredrika relies only on intellect, rejecting intuition, and this has made relations with her new colleagues tense, to say the least. Yet it is Fredrika who solves a series of horrific crimes that have left her colleagues mystified and helpless.

Enjoy a preview of Kristina Ohlsson's *Unwanted* and meet Fredrika Bergman, the leading investigative analyst in Sweden's police force.

Available as a hardcover
and eBook from
EMILY BESTLER BOOKS

Excerpt from
Unwanted © 2012
by Kristina Ohlsson

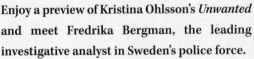

Sweden

It was in the middle of that summer of endless rain that the first child went missing. It all started on a Tuesday, an odd sort of day that could have passed like any other, but ended up being one that profoundly changed the lives of a number of people. Henry Lindgren was among them.

It was the third Tuesday in July, and Henry was doing an extra shift on the X2000 express train from Gothenburg to Stockholm. He had worked as a conductor for Swedish National Railways for more years than he cared to remember, and couldn't really imagine what would become of him the day they forced him to retire. What would he do with all his time, alone as he was?

Perhaps it was Henry Lindgren's eye for detail that meant he was later able to recall so well the young woman who was to lose her child on that journey. The young woman with red hair, in a green linen blouse and open-toed sandals that revealed toenails painted blue. If Henry and his wife had had a daughter, she would presumably have looked just like that, because his wife had been the reddest of redheads.

The red-haired woman's little girl, however, was not the least like her mother, Henry noted as he clipped their tickets just after they pulled out of the station in Gothenburg. The girl's hair was a dark, chestnut brown and fell in such soft waves that it looked almost unreal. It landed lightly on her shoulders and then somehow came forward to frame her little face. Her skin was darker than her mother's, but her eyes were big and blue. There were little clusters of freckles on the bridge of her nose, making her face look less doll-like. Henry smiled at her as he went past. She smiled back shyly. Henry thought the girl looked tired. She turned her head away and looked out of the window.

"Lilian, take your shoes off if you're going to put your feet up on the seat," Henry heard the woman say to the child just as he turned to clip the next passenger's ticket.

When he turned back toward them, the child had kicked off her mauve sandals and tucked her feet up under her. The sandals were still there on the floor after she disappeared.

It was rather a rowdy journey from Gothenburg to Stockholm. A lot of the passengers had traveled down to Sweden's second city to see a world-class star in concert at the Ullevi Stadium. They were now returning on the morning service on which Henry was the conductor.

First, Henry had problems in coach 5 where two young men had thrown up on their seats. They were hung over from the previous night's partying at Ullevi, and Henry had to dash off for cleaning fluid and a damp cloth. At about the same time, two younger girls got into a fight in coach three. A blond girl accused a brunette of trying to steal her boyfriend. Henry tried to mediate, but to no avail, and the train did not really settle down until they were past Skövde. Then all the trouble-makers finally dozed off, and Henry had a cup of coffee with Nellie, who worked in the buffet car. On his way back, Henry noticed that the red-haired woman and her daughter were asleep, too.

From then on it was a fairly uneventful journey until they were nearing Stockholm. It was the deputy conductor Arvid Melin who made the announcement just before they got to Flemingsberg, twenty kilometers or so short of the capital. The driver had been notified of a signaling problem on the final stretch to Stockholm Central, and there would therefore be a delay of five or possibly ten minutes.

While they were waiting at Flemingsberg, Henry noticed the

red-haired woman quickly get off the train, alone. He watched
her surreptitiously from the window of the tiny compartment in
coach 6 that was reserved for the train crew. He saw her take a
few determined steps across the platform, over to the other side
where it was less crowded. She took something out of her hand-
bag; could it be a mobile phone? He assumed the child must still
be asleep in her seat. She certainly had been a little while ago,
as the train thundered through Katrineholm. Henry sighed to
himself. What on earth was he thinking of, spying on attractive
women?

Henry looked away and started on the crossword in his
magazine. He was to wonder time and again what would have
happened if he had kept his eye on the woman on the platform.
It made no difference how many people tried to persuade him
that he couldn't possibly have known, that he mustn't reproach
himself. Henry was, and forever would be, convinced that his
eagerness to solve a crossword had destroyed a young mother's
life. There was absolutely nothing he could do to turn back the
clock.

Henry was still busy with his crossword when he heard
Arvid's voice on the public-address system. All passengers were
to return to their seats. The train was now ready to continue on
its way to Stockholm.

Afterward, nobody could recall seeing a young woman run
after the train. But she must have done so, because it was only
a few minutes later that Henry took an urgent call in the staff
compartment. A young woman who had been sitting in seat 6,
coach 2, with her daughter had been left behind on the platform in Flemingsberg when the train set off again, and was now
in a taxi on her way to central Stockholm. Her little daughter
was therefore alone on the train.

"Bugger it," said Henry as he hung up.

Why could he never delegate a single duty without something going wrong? Why could he never have a moment's peace?

They never even discussed stopping the train at an intermediate station, since it was so close to its final destination. Henry made his way briskly to coach 2, and realized it must have been the red-haired woman he'd been watching on the platform who had missed the train, since he recognized her daughter, now sitting alone. He reported back to the communication center on his mobile phone that the girl was still asleep, and that there was surely no need to upset her with the news of her mother's absence before they got to Stockholm. There was general agreement, and Henry promised to look after the girl personally when the train pulled in. *Personally.* A word that would ring in Henry's head for a long time.

Just as the train went through the Söder station on the southern outskirts, the girls in coach 3 started scuffling and screaming again. The sound of breaking glass reached Henry's ears as a door slid open for a passenger to move between coaches 2 and 3, and he had to leave the sleeping child. He made an urgent and agitated call to Arvid on the two-way radio.

"Arvid, come straight to coach three!" he barked.

Not a sound from his colleague.

The train had come to a halt with its characteristic hiss, like the heavy, wheezing breath of an old person, before Henry managed to separate the two girls.

"Whore!" shrieked the blond one.

"Slut!" retorted her friend.

"What a terrible way to behave," said an elderly lady who had just gotten up to retrieve her case from the rack above.

Henry edged swiftly past people who had started queuing in the aisle to get off, and called over his shoulder, "Just make sure you leave the train right away, you two!"

As he spoke, he was already on his way to coach two. He just hoped the child hadn't woken up. But he had never been far away, after all.

Henry forged his way onward, knocking into several people as he covered the short distance back, and afterward he swore he'd been away no more than three minutes.

But the number of minutes, however small, changed nothing.

When he got back to coach 2, the sleeping child was gone. Her mauve sandals were still there on the floor. And the train was disgorging onto the platform all those people who had traveled under Henry Lindgren's protection from Gothenburg to Stockholm.

Alex Recht had been a policeman for more than a quarter of a century. He therefore felt he had every justification for claiming to have wide experience of police work, to have built up over the years a not insignificant level of professional competence, and to have developed a finely honed sense of intuition. He possessed, he was often told, a good gut instinct.

Few things were more important to a policeman than gut instinct. It was the hallmark of a skilled police officer, the ultimate way of identifying who was made of the right stuff and who wasn't. Gut instinct was never a substitute for facts, but it could complement them. When all the facts were on the table, all the pieces of the puzzle identified, the trick was to understand what you were looking at and assemble the fragments of knowledge you had in front of you into a whole.

"Many are called, but few are chosen," Alex's father had said in the speech he had made to his son when he got his first police appointment.

Alex's father had in actual fact been hoping his son would go into the church, like all the other firstborn sons in the family before him. He found it very hard to resign himself to the fact that his son had chosen the police in preference.

"Being a police officer involves a sort of calling, too," Alex said in an attempt to mollify him.

His father thought about that for a few months, and then let it be known that he intended to accept and respect his son's choice of profession. Perhaps the matter was also simplified somewhat by the fact that Alex's brother later decided to enter the priesthood. At any rate, Alex was eternally grateful to his brother.

Alex liked working with people who, just like him, felt a particular sense of vocation in the job. He liked working with people who shared his intuition and a well-developed feeling for what was fact and what was nonsense.

Maybe, he thought to himself as he sat at the wheel on the way to Stockholm Central, maybe that was why he couldn't really warm to his new colleague Fredrika Bergman. She seemed to consider herself neither called to, nor particularly good at, her job. But then he didn't really expect her police career to last very long.

Alex glanced surreptitiously at the figure in the passenger seat beside him. She was sitting up incredibly straight. He had initially wondered if she had a military background. He had even hoped that might be the case. But however often he went through her CV, he couldn't find a single line to hint that she had spent so much as an hour in the armed forces. Alex had sighed. Then she must be a gymnast, that was all it could be, because no normal woman who had done nothing more exciting than go to university would ever be that bloody straight backed.

Alex cleared his throat quietly and wondered if he ought to say anything about the case before they got there. After all, Fredrika had never had to deal with this sort of business before. Their eyes met briefly and then Alex turned his gaze back to the road.

"Lot of traffic today," he muttered.

As if there were days when inner-city Stockholm was empty of cars.

In his many years in the police, Alex had dealt with a fair number of missing children. His work on these cases had gradually convinced him of the truth of the saying: "Children don't vanish, people lose them." In almost every case, *almost* every case, behind every lost child there was a lost parent. Some lax individual who in Alex's view should never have had children in the first place. It needn't necessarily be someone with a harmful lifestyle or alcohol problems. It could just as well be someone who worked far too much, who was out with friends far too often and far too late, or someone who simply didn't pay enough attention to their child. If children took up the space in adults' lives that they should, they would go missing far less often. At least that was what Alex had concluded.

The clouds hung thick and dark in the sky and a faint rumble presaged thunder as they got out of the car. The air was incredibly heavy and humid. It was the sort of day when you longed for rain and thunder to make the air more breathable. A flash of lightning etched itself dully on the clouds somewhere over the Old Town. There was another storm approaching.

Alex and Fredrika hurried in through the main entrance to Stockholm Central. Alex took a call from the mobile of the third member of the investigating team, Peder Rydh, to say he was on his way. Alex was relieved. It wouldn't have felt right starting an investigation like this with no one but a desk jockey like Fredrika.

It was after half past three by the time they got to platform 17, where the train had pulled in, to become the subject of a standard crime scene investigation. Swedish National Railways had been informed that no precise time could be given for the train to be put back in service, which in due course led to the late running of a good many other trains that day. There were only a few people on the platform not in police uniform. Alex guessed that the red-haired woman looking exhausted but composed, sitting on a large, blue plastic box marked SAND, was the missing child's mother. Alex sensed intuitively that the woman was not one of those parents who lose their children. He swallowed hastily. If the child hadn't been lost, it had been abducted. If it had been abducted, that complicated matters significantly.

Alex told himself to take it easy. He still knew too little about the case not to keep an open mind.

A young, uniformed officer came along the platform to Alex and Fredrika. His handshake was firm but a little damp, his look somewhat glazed and unfocused. He introduced himself simply as Jens. Alex guessed that he was a recent graduate of the police-training college and that this was his first case. Lack of practical experience was frightening when new police officers took up their first posts. One could see them radiating confusion and sometimes pure panic in their first six months. Alex wondered if the young man whose hand he was shaking couldn't be said to be bordering on panic. He was probably wondering in turn what on earth Alex was doing there. DCIs rarely, if ever, turned up to conduct interviews themselves. Or at any rate, not at this early stage in a case.

Alex was about to explain his presence when Jens started to speak, in rapid bursts.

"The alarm wasn't raised until thirty minutes after the train got in," he reported in a shrill voice. "And by then, nearly all the passengers had left the platform. Well, except for these."

He gave a sweeping wave, indicating of a clump of people standing a little way beyond the woman Alex had identified as the child's mother. Alex glanced at his watch. It was twenty to four. The child would soon have been missing for an hour and a half.

"There's been a complete search of the train. She isn't anywhere. The child, I mean, a six-year-old girl. She's not anywhere. And nobody seems to have seen her, either. At least nobody we've spoken to. And all their luggage is still there. The girl didn't take anything with her. Not even her shoes. They were still on the floor under her seat."

The first raindrops hit the roof above them. The thunder was rumbling somewhere closer now. Alex didn't think he'd ever known a worse summer.

"Is that the girl's mother sitting over there?" asked Fredrika with a discreet nod toward the red-haired woman.

"Yes, that's right," said the young policeman. "Her name's Sara Sebastiansson. She says she's not going home until we find the girl."

Alex gave an inward sigh. Of course the red-haired woman was the child's mother. He didn't need to ask such things, he knew them anyway, he *sensed* them. Fredrika was entirely lacking in that sort of intuition. She asked about everything and she questioned even more. Alex felt his irritation level rising. Detecting simply didn't work that way. He only hoped she would soon realize how wrong she was for the profession she had decided was suitable for her.

"Why did it take thirty minutes for the police to be alerted?" Fredrika demanded.

Alex immediately pricked up his ears. Fredrika had finally asked a relevant question.

Jens braced himself. Up to that point, he had had answers to all the questions the senior police officers had asked him since they arrived.

"Well, it's a bit of an odd story," Jens began, and Alex could see he was trying not to stare at Fredrika. "The train was held at Flemingsberg for longer than usual, and the mother got off to make a phone call. She left her little girl on the train because she was asleep."

Alex nodded thoughtfully. *Children don't vanish, people lose them.* Perhaps he had misjudged Sara the redhead.

"So anyway, a girl came up to her, to Sara that is, on the platform and asked her to help with a dog that was sick. And then she missed the train. She rang the train people right away—a member of the staff at Flemingsberg helped her—to tell them that her child was on the train and that she was going to take a taxi straight to Stockholm Central."

Alex was frowning as he listened.

"The child had gone by the time the train stopped at Stockholm, and the conductor and some of the other crew searched for her. People were flooding off the train, see, and hardly any of the passengers bothered to help. A Securitas guard who normally hangs round outside the Burger King downstairs gave them a hand with the search. Then the mother, I mean Sara over there, got here in the taxi and was told her daughter was missing. They went on searching; they thought the girl must have woken up and been one of the first off the train. But they couldn't find her anywhere. So then they rang the police. But we haven't found her, either."

"Have they put out a call over the public-address system in the station?" asked Fredrika. "I mean in case she managed to get off the platform and onto the concourse?"

Jens nodded meekly and then shook his head. Yes, an announcement had been made. More police and volunteers were currently searching the whole station. Local radio would be issuing an appeal to road users in the city center to keep an eye out for the girl. The taxi firms would be contacted. If the girl had walked off on her own, she couldn't have gotten far.

But she had not been spotted yet.

Fredrika nodded slowly. Alex looked at the mother sitting on the big blue box. She looked shattered. Done for.

"Put out the announcement in other languages, not just Swedish," said Fredrika.

Her male colleagues looked at her with raised eyebrows.

"There are a lot of people hanging about here who don't have Swedish as their mother tongue, but who might have seen something. Make the announcement in English, too. German and French, if they can. Maybe Arabic, as well."

Alex nodded approvingly and sent Jens a look that told him to do as Fredrika suggested. Jens hurried off, probably quailing at the prospect of somehow getting hold of an Arabic speaker. Cascades of rain were coming down on those gathered on the platform, and the rumbling had turned into mighty claps of thunder. It was a wretched day in a wretched summer.

Peder Rydh came dashing along the platform just as Jens was leaving it. Peder stared at Fredrika's beige, double-breasted jacket. Had the woman no concept at all of the way you signaled that you were part of the police when you weren't in uniform? Peder himself nodded graciously to the colleagues he passed on his way and waved his identity badge about a bit so they would realize he was one of them. He found it hard to resist the urge to thump a few of the younger talents on the back. He had loved his years in the patrol car, of course, but he was very happy indeed to have landed a job on the plainclothes side.

Alex gave Peder a nod as they caught sight of each other, and his look expressed something close to gratitude for his colleague's presence.

"I was on my way from a meeting on the edge of town when I got the message that the child was missing, so I thought I'd pick up Fredrika on the way and come straight here," Alex explained briefly to Peder. "I'm not really planning to stick around, just wanted to get out for a bit of fresh air," he went on, and gave his colleague a knowing look.

"You mean you wanted to get your feet on the ground as a change from being chained to your desk?" grinned Peder, and received a weary nod in reply.

In spite of the significant age gap between them, the two men were entirely in agreement on that point. You were never so far up in the hierarchy that you didn't need to see the real shit. And you were never as far from reality as when you were behind your desk.

Both men assumed, however, that Fredrika did not share this view, and therefore said nothing more about it.

"Okay," said Alex instead. "Here's what we'll do. Fredrika can take the initial interview with the child's mother, and you, Peder, can talk to the train crew and also find out if any of the other passengers who're still here can give you any information. We should really play it by the book and interview in pairs, but I can't see that there's time to organize that just now."

Fredrika was very happy with this division of duties, but thought she could detect some dissatisfaction in Peder's face.

Dissatisfaction that she, not he, would get to tackle the mother of the missing child. Alex must have seen it, too, as he added, "The only reason Fredrika's dealing with the mother is that she's a woman. It tends to make things a bit easier."

Peder instantly looked a little more cheerful.

"Okay, see you back at the station later," said Alex gruffly. "I'm off back there now."

Fredrika sighed. *"The only reason Fredrika's dealing with . . ."* It was always the same. Every decision to entrust her with a task had to be defended. She was a foreign body in a foreign universe. Her whole presence was questionable and demanded constant explanation. Fredrika felt so indignant that she forgot to reflect on the fact that Alex had not only entrusted her with interviewing the mother, but also let her do it alone. She was virtually counting the days until her time on Alex Recht's investigation team was over. She was planning to finish her probationary period and then leave. There were other agencies where her qualifications were more desirable, albeit less urgently needed.

I shall look over my shoulder one last time and then never look back again, thought Fredrika, seeing in her mind's eye the day she would stride out of the police building, or HQ, as her colleagues generally called it, on Kungsholmen. Then Fredrika turned her attention to a more imminent task. To the missing child.

She introduced herself politely to Sara Sebastiansson and was surprised by the strength of the woman's handshake. It belied the anxiety and exhaustion in her face. Fredrika also noted that Sara kept pulling down the sleeves of her top. It looked like a sort of tic, or habit, something she did all the time. It was almost as if she was trying to hide her forearms.

Maybe an attempt to conceal injuries she'd gotten when she was defending herself, thought Fredrika. If Sara had a husband who hit her, that was information to be brought to the team's attention as soon as possible.

But there were other questions to be asked first.

"We can go inside if you like," Fredrika said to Sara. "We needn't stand out here in the rain."

"I'm all right here," said Sara in a voice not far from tears.

Fredrika pondered this for a moment and then said, "If you feel you have to be here for your daughter, you have my absolute assurance that she'd be noticed by everybody else here."

What's more, Fredrika felt like adding, *it's not particularly likely that your daughter will turn up right here and now,* but she left the thought unsaid.

"Lilian," said Sara.

"Sorry?"

"My daughter's called Lilian. And I don't want to leave this spot."

She underlined what she was saying by shaking her head.

Fredrika knew herself that she found it hard to be personal when she was on duty. She often failed dismally. In that respect, she was a classic desk type. She liked reading, writing, and analyzing. All forms of interrogation and conversation felt so alien, so hard to deal with. She would sometimes watch with pure fascination as Alex reached out a hand and laid it on someone's shoulder as he was talking to them. Fredrika would never do that, and what was more, she didn't want to be patted herself, either, be it on the arm or on the shoulder. She felt physically unwell whenever any male colleague at work tried to "lighten the mood" by slapping her on the back too hard or prodding her in the middle. She didn't like that sort of physical contact at all. And most people realized this. But not all.

Fredrika gave a slight shiver just as Sara's voice interrupted her very private musings.

"Why didn't she take her shoes?"

"Sorry?"

"Lilian's sandals were still there on the floor by her seat. She must have been in a terrible state about something, otherwise she'd never have gone off in her bare feet. And never without saying something to somebody, asking for help."

"Not even if she woke up and found she was all alone? Maybe she panicked and dashed off the train?"

Sara shook her head.

"Lilian's not like that. That's not how we brought her up. We taught her to act and think in a practical way. She would have asked someone sitting nearby. The lady across the aisle from us, for example, we'd chatted to her a bit on the way."

Fredrika saw her chance to divert the conversation on to another subject.

"You say 'we'?"

"Yes?"

"You say that's not how 'we' brought her up. Are you referring to yourself and your husband?"

Sara fixed her gaze on a spot above Fredrika's shoulder.

"Lilian's father and I have separated, but yes, it's my ex-husband I brought up Lilian with."

"Have you got joint custody?" asked Fredrika.

"The separation's so new for us all," Sara said slowly. "We haven't really gotten into a routine. Lilian sometimes stays with him on weekends, but mostly she lives with me. We'll have to see how it goes, later."

Sara took a deep breath, and as she breathed out, her lower lip was trembling. Her ashen skin stood out against her red hair. Her long arms were crossed tightly on her chest. Fredrika looked at Sara's painted toenails. Blue. How unusual.

"Did you argue about who Lilian was going to live with?" Fredrika probed cautiously.

Sara gave a start.

"You think Gabriel's taken her?" she said, looking Fredrika straight in the eye.

Fredrika assumed Gabriel must be the ex-husband.

"We don't think anything," she said quickly. "I just have to investigate all possible scenarios for . . . I just have to try to understand what might have happened to her. To Lilian."

Sara's shoulders slumped a little. She bit her lower lip and stared hard at the ground.

"Gabriel and I . . . have had . . . still have . . . our differences. Not so long ago we had a row about Lilian. But he's never harmed her. Never ever."

Again Fredrika saw Sara pulling at the sleeves of her top. Her rapid assessment was that Sara would not tell her then and there whether she had been abused by her ex-husband or not. She would have to check for officially lodged complaints when she got back to HQ. And, in any event, they would certainly have to speak to the ex-husband.

"Could you tell me more precisely what happened on the platform at Flemingsberg?" Fredrika asked, hoping she was now steering the conversation in a direction Sara would find more comfortable.

Sara nodded several times but said nothing. Fredrika hoped she wasn't going to start crying, because tears were something she found very hard to deal with. Not privately, but professionally.

"I got off the train to make a call," Sara began hesitantly. "I rang a friend."

Fredrika, distracted by the rain, checked herself. *A friend?*

"And why didn't you ring from your seat?"

"I didn't want to wake Lilian," came Sara's quick response.

A little too quick. What was more, she had told the policeman she spoke to earlier that she'd gotten off the train because she was in the so-called quiet coach.

"She was so tired," whispered Sara. "We go to Gothenburg to visit my parents. I think she was getting a cold; she usually never sleeps for the whole journey."

"Ah, I see," said Fredrika, and paused for a minute before going on. "So it wasn't that you didn't want Lilian to hear the conversation?"

Sara admitted it almost immediately.

"No, I didn't want Lilian to hear the conversation," she said quietly. "My friend and I have . . . only just met. And it would be a bad idea to let her find out about him at this stage."

Because then she'd tell her dad, who was presumably still beating up her mum even though they'd separated, thought Fredrika to herself.

"We only talked for a couple of minutes. Less than that, I think. I said we were almost there, and he could come round to my place later this evening, once Lilian was in bed."

"All right, and what happened next?"

Sara pulled her shoulders back and sighed heavily. The body language told Fredrika they were about to discuss something she found really painful to remember.

"It made no sense at all, not any of it," Sara said dully. "It was completely absurd."

She shook her head wearily.

"A woman came up to me. Or a girl, you might say. Quite tall, thin, looked a bit the worse for wear. Waving her arms and shouting something about her dog being sick. I suppose she came up to me because I was standing separately from the other people on the platform. She said she'd been coming down the escalator with the dog when it suddenly collapsed and started having a seizure."

"A fit? The dog?"

"Yes, that was what she said. The dog was lying there having a fit and she needed help to get it back up the escalator again. I've had dogs all my life, until a few years ago. And I could honestly see what a state the girl was in. So I helped her."

Sara fell silent and Fredrika considered what she'd said, rubbing her hands together.

"Didn't you think about the risk of missing the train?"

For the first time in their conversation, Sara's tone was sharp and her eyes blazed.

"When I got off, I asked the conductor how long the train would be stopping there. He said at least ten minutes. At least."

Sara held up her hands and spread her long, narrow fingers wide. Ten fingers, ten minutes. Her hands were shaking slightly. Her lower lip was quivering again.

"Ten minutes," she whispered. "That was why I helped the girl shove the dog up the escalator. I thought—I *knew*—I had time."

Fredrika tried to breathe calmly.

"Did you see the train leave?"

"We'd just gotten to the top of the escalator with the dog," said Sara, her voice unsteady. "We'd just gotten the dog back up when I turned round and saw the train starting to pull out."

Her breathing was labored and her eyes were on Fredrika.

"I couldn't believe my fucking eyes," she said, and a single tear ran down her cheek. "It was like being in a horror film. I ran down the escalator, ran like mad after the train. But it didn't stop. It didn't stop!"

Although Fredrika had no children of her own, Sara's words aroused a genuine feeling of anguish in her.

She felt something akin to a stomachache.

"One of the staff at the Flemingsberg station helped me get in touch with the train. And then I took a taxi to Stockholm Central."

"What was the girl with the dog doing while this was happening?"

Sara wiped the corner of her eye.

"It was a bit odd. She just sort of made off, all of a sudden. She bundled the dog up onto some kind of parcel trolley that had been left there at the top of the escalator, and went out though the station entrance. I didn't see her after that."

Sara and Fredrika stood for a while saying nothing, each absorbed in her own thoughts. It was Sara's voice that broke the silence.

"And you know what, I wasn't really too worried once I'd gotten through to the train. It felt pretty irrational to get worked up about a little thing like Lilian being by herself for that last bit of the journey from Flemingsberg to Stockholm."

Sara moistened her lips, and then cried openly for the first time.

"I even sat back in the taxi. Closed my eyes and relaxed. I *relaxed* while some bloody sick bastard took my little girl."

Fredrika realized this was a pain she had no chance of alleviating. With great reluctance she did what she would never normally do: she reached out a hand and stroked Sara's arm.

Then she realized it had stopped raining. Lilian had been missing for another hour.

The story continues in *Unwanted*, available in hardcover and eBook from EMILY BESTLER BOOKS.

ALSO BY SPENCER QUINN

Thereby Hangs a Tail
To Fetch a Thief
The Dog Who Knew Too Much
A Fistful of Collars (September 2012)

DOG ON IT

by Spencer Quinn

Introducing Chet and Bernie

Meet Chet, the wise and lovable canine narrator of the Chet and Bernie mystery series, who works alongside Bernie, a down-on-his-luck private investigator. Chet might have flunked out of police school ("I'd been the best leaper in K-9 class, which had led to all the trouble in a way I couldn't remember exactly, although blood was involved"), but he's a detective through and through. Full of heart and occasionally prone to mischief, Chet is intensely loyal to Bernie, though somewhat confused by the all-too-human issues that distract him—divorce, cash flow, treating people badly, and child custody among others. It's the smaller things in life that Chet really knows how to appreciate—finding a chew toy he'd buried, riding in the car, getting a great back scratch, and sinking his teeth into something. Humorous and full of insight into the bond between dog and man, Chet truly sums up why dog is man's best friend. From his perspective, crime has never been so much fun.

Read on for a look at the first chapter of Spencer Quinn's *Dog on It* where you will first meet Chet and see the world from his point of view.

Currently available as a paperback and eBook from **ATRIA** BOOKS

Excerpt from
Dog on It
© 2011 by
Spencer Quinn

*The American
Southwest*

I could smell him—or rather the booze on his breath—before he even opened the door, but my sense of smell is pretty good, probably better than yours. The key scratched against the lock, finally found the slot. The door opened and in, with a little stumble, came Bernie Little, founder and part owner (his ex-wife, Leda, walked off with the rest) of the Little Detective Agency. I'd seen him look worse, but not often.

He mustered a weak smile. "Hey, Chet."

I raised my tail and let it thump down on the rug, just so, sending a message.

"I'm a little late, sorry. Need to go out?"

Why would that be? Just because my back teeth were floating? But then I thought, What the hell, the poor guy, and I went over and pressed my head against the side of his leg. He scratched between my ears, really digging his fingers in, the way I like. Bliss. How about a little more, down the back of the neck? I hunched my shoulders a bit, giving him the idea. Ah, nice. Very nice.

We went outside, me and Bernie. There were three trees out front, my favorite being a big shady one just perfect for napping under. I lifted my leg against it. Wow. Hadn't realized I was that close to desperation. The night filled with splashing sounds and I zoned out a little, listening to them. I managed to stop the flow—not easy—and save some for dampening the rock at the end of the driveway and the wooden fence that separated our property from old man Heydrich's next door, plus a squirt or two between the slats. Only doing my job, but don't get me started on old man Heydrich.

Bernie was gazing up at the sky. A beautiful night—soft

breeze, lots of stars, lights twinkling down the canyon, and what was this? A new tennis ball on the lawn. I went over and sniffed it. Not one of mine, not anyone's I knew.

"Wanna play fetch?"

I pawed the thing. How did it get here? Cooped up all day, but I'd kept an ear cocked; except for when I dozed off, of course.

"Bring it here, Chet."

I didn't want to, not with this stranger's smell on it.

"Come on."

But I never said no to Bernie. I gave the ball a lick or two, making it mine, then took it over to Bernie and dropped it at his feet. Bernie reared back and threw the ball up the canyon road.

"Uh-oh—where'd it go?"

Where'd it go? He really couldn't see it? That never failed to surprise me, how poorly he saw after the sun went down. I tore after the ball, bouncing up the middle of the road in plain sight, got my back feet way forward and sprang, totally airborne, snaring it on the short hop, the way I like, then wheeling around in one skidding motion and racing full speed, head low, ears flattened by the wind I was making, and dropped it at Bernie's feet, putting on the brakes at the last moment. If you know something more fun than this, let me in on the secret.

"Got it on the short hop? Couldn't tell from here."

I wagged my tail, that quick one-two wag meaning yes, not the over-the-top one that wags itself and can mean lots of things, some of which I'm not too clear on myself.

"Nice." He picked up the ball and was rearing back again when a car came slowly down the street and stopped in front of us.

The window slid down and a woman leaned out. "Is this thirteen-three-oh-nine?"

Bernie nodded.

"I'm looking for Bernie Little, the detective."

"You found him."

She opened the door, started to get out, then saw me. "Is the dog all right?"

Bernie stiffened. I felt it; he was standing right beside me. "Depends what you mean."

"You know, is he safe, does he bite? I'm not that comfortable around dogs."

"He won't bite you."

Of course I wouldn't. But the idea was planted in my head, for sure. I could tell by all the saliva suddenly pooling in my mouth.

"Thanks. You never know about dogs."

Bernie said something under his breath, too low for even me to hear; but I knew I liked it, whatever it was.

She got out of the car, a tall woman with long fair hair and a smell of flowers and lemons, plus a trace of another smell that reminded me of what happens only sometimes to the females in my world. What would that be like, having it turned on all the time? Probably drive you crazy. I glanced at Bernie, watching her, patting his hair into place. Oh, Bernie.

"I'm not sure where to begin. Nothing like this has ever happened to me."

"Nothing like what?"

She wrung her hands. Hands are the weirdest things about humans, and the best: you can find out just about everything you need to know by watching them. "I live over on El Presidente." She waved vaguely.

El Presidente: Was that the one where the sewer pipes were still going in? I was bad on street names—except our own, Mesquite Road—but why not? I didn't need them to find my way.

"My name's Cynthia Chambliss. I work with a woman you helped."

"Who?"

"Angela DiPesto."

Mercy. I remembered endless nights parked in front of motels up and down the state. We hated divorce work, me and Bernie, never even accepted any in the old days. But now we were having cash-flow problems, as Bernie put it. The truth was, I didn't really know what "cash-flow problems" meant, but whatever they were, they woke Bernie in the night, made him get up and pace around, sometimes lighting a cigarette, even though he'd worked so hard to stop.

Bernie didn't commit to anything about Angela DiPesto, just gave one of those little nods of his. Bernie was a great nodder. He had several different nods I could think of off the top of my head, all very readable once you knew what to look for. This particular nod meant: strike one.

"The fact is, Angie spoke of you highly—how you stuck it to that creep of a husband." She gave herself a little shake. I can do that way, way better. "So when this happened, and you being practically in the neighborhood and all . . . anyway, here I am." She rocked back and forth slightly, the way humans do when they're very nervous.

"When what happened?"

"This thing with Madison. She's disappeared."

"Madison is your daughter?"

"Didn't I say that? Sorry. I'm just so upset, I don't know what I'm . . ."

Her eyes glistened up. This was always pretty interesting, the crying thing; not the sound—I could relate to that—but the waterworks, as Bernie called them, especially when Leda was on the producing end. They get upset, humans, and then water comes out of their eyes, especially the women. What is that all about? Bernie gazed down at the ground, shuffled his feet; he didn't have a handle on it, either, although I'd once seen water seeping out of his own eyes, namely the day Leda had packed up all Charlie's things. Charlie was their kid—Bernie and Leda's—and now lived with Leda except for visits. We missed him, me and Bernie.

This woman—Cynthia? Chambliss? whatever her name was—the truth is, I have trouble catching names at first, sometimes miss other things, too, unless I have a real good view of the speaker's face—took a tissue from a little bag she carried and dabbed at her eyes. "Sorry."

"Nothing to be sorry for. How long has Madison been missing?"

The woman started to answer, but at that moment I heard something rustling in the bushes on the far side of the driveway. The next thing I knew, I was in the bushes myself, sniffing around, maybe even digging, but only the littlest bit. Some kind of smell was in the air, frog or toad, or . . . uh-oh: snake. I didn't like snakes, didn't like them at—

"Chet? You're not digging in there, are you?"

I backed out of the bushes, trotted over to Bernie. Oops—my tail was down, tucked back in a guilty manner. I stuck it right up, high and innocent.

"Good boy." He patted my head. Thump thump. Ah.

The woman was tapping her foot on the ground. "So you're saying you won't help me?"

Bernie took a deep breath. His eyes looked tired. The booze was wearing off. He'd be sleepy very soon. I was feeling a bit sleepy myself. Plus a little taste of something might be nice. Were there any of those rawhide chew strips left in the top drawer by the kitchen sink, the ones with that Southwestern flav—

"That's not exactly what I said. Your daughter didn't come home from school today. That makes her gone, what, not yet eight hours? The police won't even open a missing-persons file till a full day's gone by."

Eight hours I had trouble with, but a full day I knew very well, from when the sun rose over the hills behind the garage to when it went down behind the hills on the other side.

"But you're not the police."

"True, and we don't always agree, but I agree on this. You say Madison's a sophomore in high school? So she's what? Sixteen?"

"Fifteen. She's in the gifted program."

"In my experience, fifteen-year-olds sometimes forget to call home, especially when they're doing something impulsive, like going to the movies, or hanging out, or partying from time to time."

"It's a school night."

"Even on school nights."

"I told you—she's gifted."

"So was Billie Holiday."

"I'm sorry?" The woman looked confused; the confused human face is almost as ugly as the angry one. I didn't get the Billie Holiday thing, either, but at least I knew who she was—this singer Bernie listened to, especially when he was in one of his brooding moods.

But even if no one got what he was talking about, Bernie seemed pleased with himself, like he'd scored some point. I could tell by the smile that crossed his face, a little one, quickly gone. "Tell you what. If you don't hear from her by morning, give me a call." He held out his card.

She gave the card a hostile look, didn't touch it. "By morning? Seventy-six percent of disappearances are solved in the first twelve hours, or they're not . . ." Her eyes got wet again, and her voice sounded like something was choking her throat. ". . . solved at all."

"Where'd you hear that?"

"I didn't *hear* it. I looked it up on the Internet before I drove over. What you don't seem to understand is that Madison has never done anything like this and never would. Maybe if you won't help, you can recommend someone who will."

Recommend another agency? Had this ever happened before? I couldn't read the look on Bernie's face at all.

"If it's money you're worried about, I'm prepared to pay whatever you charge, plus a big bonus the moment you find her." She reached into her bag, pulled out a roll, peeled off some bills. "How's five hundred in advance?"

Bernie's eyes shifted over to the money and stayed there, his face now readable to anyone from any distance, his mind on cash flow. "I'd like to see her room first." When Bernie caved, he did it quickly and all at once. I'd seen it with Leda a thousand times.

Cynthia handed over the money. "Follow me."

Bernie stuffed the bills deep in his pocket. I ran over to our car—an old Porsche convertible, the body sandblasted, waiting a long time now for a new coat of paint—and jumped over the passenger-side door and into my seat.

"Hey. Did you see what your dog just did?"

Bernie nodded, the proud, confident nod, my favorite. "They call him Chet the Jet." Well, Bernie does, anyway, although not often.

A coyote shrieked in the canyon, not far from the back of the house. I'd have to deal with that later. I no longer felt tired at all. And Bernie, turning the key in the ignition, looked the same: rarin' to go. We thrived on work, me and Bernie.

The story continues in *Dog on It*, available in paperback and eBook from ATRIA BOOKS.

ALSO BY M. J. ROSE

Fiction

Lip Service

In Fidelity

Flesh Tones

Sheet Music

Lying in Bed

The Halo Effect

The Delilah Complex

The Venus Fix

The Reincarnationist

The Memoirist

The Hypnotist

Nonfiction

Buzz Your Book (with Douglas Clegg)

The Book of Lost Fragrances

by M. J. Rose

Introducing Jac L'Etoile

This mythologist, television personality, and author has always been haunted by the past, memories infused with the exotic scents that she grew up around as the heir to a storied French perfume company. Fleeing the pain of those remembrances—and the suicide of her mother—by moving to America, she's left the company in the hands of her brother, Robbie. But when Robbie hints at an earth-shattering discovery in the family archives, and then suddenly goes missing—leaving a dead body in his wake—Jac is plunged into a world she thought she'd left behind.

Read on to meet Jac L'Etoile in one of her first scenes in M. J. Rose's *The Book of Lost Fragrances.*

Available as a hardcover and eBook from **ATRIA** BOOKS

Excerpt from *The Book of Lost Fragrances*
© 2012 by M. J. Rose

France

WHEN JAC L'ETOILE was fourteen years old, mythology saved her life. She remembered everything about that year. Especially the things she'd tried to forget. Those she remembered in the most detail. It was always like that, wasn't it?

The teenager waiting for her now, outside the TV studio on West Forty-ninth Street, couldn't be much older than fourteen. Gangly, awkward, but excited and jittery like a young colt, she stepped forward and held out a copy of Jac's book, *Mythfinders*.

"Can I have your autograph, Miss L'Etoile?"

Jac had just been on a network morning talk show promoting her book, but she wasn't by any means a celebrity. Her cable show, also titled *Mythfinders*—exploring the genesis of legends— claimed under a million viewers, so encounters like this were both unexpected and gratifying.

The town car she'd ordered idled at the curb, the driver standing at the ready by the passenger door. But it didn't matter if she was a little late. No one but ghosts waited for her where she was going.

"What's your name?" Jac asked.

"Maddy."

Jac could smell the light, lemony cologne the girl was wearing. Teenage girls and citron were forever finding each other. Uncapping the pen, Jac started to write.

"Sometimes it helps to know there really are heroes," Maddy said in a hushed voice. "That people can really do amazing things."

The noisy and crowded street across from Radio City Music Hall was an odd place for a confession, but Jac nodded and smiled at Maddy in complicity.

She'd known the same hunger far too long.

When Jac first started exploring the genesis of myths—traveling to ancient sites all over the world; visiting museums, private collections and libraries; searching the ruins of civilizations long gone—she'd imagined her findings would entertain and educate. To that end, she sought out and found the facts at the center of the great fictions, looked for and discovered the life-size versions of the giants in legends. She wrote about how celebrated deeds had in actuality been small acts, sometimes even accidents. Jac reported on how rarely the deaths of mythology's heroes were grand, metaphoric or meteoric, but instead how storytellers had exaggerated reality to create metaphors that instructed and inspired.

She believed she was debunking myths. Bringing them down to size. But she wound up doing the opposite.

The proof that myths were, in fact, based in fact—that some version of ancient heroes, gods, fates, furies and muses really had existed—gave readers and viewers hope.

And that's why they wrote Jac fan letters and thank-you notes, why Jac's TV show was in its second year, and why teenagers like Maddy asked for her autograph.

And it was why Jac felt like a fraud.

Jac knew that believing in heroes could save your life but also knew that such belief in grandiose fantasy could destroy it just as easily. She didn't tell Maddy that. Instead she finished the inscription, handed back the book, thanked her, and then slipped into the waiting car.

Forty-five minutes later the aroma of towering pines and newly blooming redbud trees informed Jac they'd reached the Sleepy Hollow Cemetery, nestled in the lush Hudson River Valley. She looked up from her reading just as the looming wrought-iron gates came into view.

As the car passed through the entrance, Jac undid and retied the ribbon that kept the wayward curls off her face. Twice. She'd been collecting ribbons since she was a child and had boxes of them: satin, grosgrain, velvet, moiré and jacquard—most found at antique stores in baskets of trimmings. There had been seven yards of this creamy satin on a water-stained spool stamped "Memorial Black."

The chauffeur drove down the cemetery's center road until he came to a fork, and then he took a right. Watching out the window for the familiar granite orb-and-cross rooftop ornament, Jac knotted and unknotted her long white scarf as the driver navigated narrow lane after lane of tombstones, mausoleums and monuments.

For the last 160 years, all of her mother's family had been buried in this Victorian cemetery that sat high on a ridge overlooking the Pocantico River. Having so many relatives asleep in this overgrown memorial park made her feel strangely at home. Uncomfortable and uneasy, but at home in this land of the dead.

The driver pulled up to a grove of locust trees, parked, and came around to open Jac's door. Her resolve fought her anxiety. She vacillated for only seconds and then got out.

Under the shade of the trees, Jac stood on the steps to the ornate Greek-style mausoleum and tried the key. She didn't remember having trouble with the lock before, but there hadn't been a river of rust flowing from the keyhole last year. Maybe the keyway had corroded. As she jiggled the blade and put pressure on the bow, she noticed how many joints between the stone blocks to the right of the door were filled with moss.

On the lintel were three bronze heads corroded by the elements. The faces—Life, Death and Immortality—peered down at her. She looked at each as she continued to jiggle the key in the lock.

The pitting that had attacked Death had, ironically, softened his expression, especially around his closed eyes. The finger he held up to his lips, silencing them forever, was rotting. So was his crown of poppies—the ancient Greek symbol for sleep.

Unlike his two elderly companions, Immortality was young, but the serpent winding around his head, tail in its mouth, was mottled with black and green deterioration. Inappropriate for an ancient icon of eternity. Only the symbol for the human soul, the butterfly in the middle of Immortality's forehead, was still pristine.

Jac's struggle with the key continued. She was almost giddy at the thought that she'd be denied entry. But the tumblers clicked solemnly, and the lock finally yielded. As she pushed it open, the door's hinges moaned like an old man. Immediately, the chalky smell of stone and stale air mixed with decayed leaves and dried wood wafted out. The "scent of the forgotten," Jac called it.

She stood on the threshold and peered inside.

The midmorning light that passed through the two stained-glass windows of purple irises saturated the interior space with a melancholy cobalt wash. It spilled over the stone angel who lay prostrate on the altar. Her face was hidden, but her grief was visible in the way her delicate marble fingers hung over the pedestal and how her wings drooped down, their tips brushing the floor.

Under each of the two windows, alabaster urns contained Jac's offerings from last year: long-dead branches of apple blossoms now withered and dried out.

In the center of the small enclosure, on a granite bench, a woman sat waiting, watching Jac, smiling a familiar, sad smile. Blue light passed through the woman's form and splashed on Jac's legs.

I was worried you weren't coming. The soft voice seemed to come from the air around the translucent specter, not from within it.

She's not real, Jac reminded herself as she stepped inside, closing the door behind her. Her mother's ghost was an aberration. A delusion of her imagination. A holdover from her illness. The last relic of those terrible times when the face Jac saw in the mirror wasn't her own—but belonged to someone unrecognizable looking back. When she'd been so sure the crayon drawings she made weren't imaginary landscapes but places she'd lived that she went searching for them. When she could hear the screams of the people she saw being buried alive . . . burned alive . . . even though no one else could.

Jac was fourteen the first time her dead mother spoke to her. Often in the hours after she'd died. Then daily, then less frequently. But after Jac left France and moved to America, she only heard her voice once a year. Here in the sepulcher on each anniversary of her mother's internment. A mother who, in essence, had abandoned her daughter too early and with too much drama. Literally *in essence*—because Audrey had died in the perfume workshop, surrounded by the most beautiful smells in the world. It would remain for Jac, who found her, a gruesome and shocking sensory memory. The scents of roses and lilies, of lavender, musk and patchouli, of vanilla, violets and verbena, of sandalwood and sage, and the image of those dead eyes open, staring into nothingness. Of an always-animated face now stilled. Of one hand outstretched in her lap—as if, at the last moment, Audrey had remembered she was leaving something important and reached out for it.

Still hugging the fresh apple blossoms she'd brought with her, Jac crossed the vault and put down the flowers on the marble floor beside the antique urn. She had a job to do here. As she lifted out last year's dead branches, they fell apart, making a mess. Kneeling, she used the edge of her hand to sweep the debris into a pile. She could have hired perpetual care for things like this yearly ritual of cleaning up, but it kept Jac occupied and tethered to something tangible and concrete during her annual visit.

She wasn't an only child, but every year she was alone in the crypt. She always reminded her brother of the date, hoping—but never assuming—that Robbie would come. Expectations lead only to disappointments. Her mother had taught her that, cautioning the little girl not to fall prey to life's tempting promises.

"Survivors," she used to tell her, "face facts." It was a tough lesson—and possibly a poisonous one—to inflict on a child who wasn't yet old enough to consider from whence the advice came: a woman who wasn't able to follow her own counsel. *You come from a family of dreamers, but there's a difference between real and pretend. Do you understand? This will help. I promise.*

But there was a difference between Jac's childhood dreams and everyone else's. Hers were full of nasty noises and ugly visions. Threats that were impossible to escape. Robbie's were fantastical. He'd believed that one day they would find the book of fragrances that their ancestor had brought back from Egypt, and use its formulas to create wonderful elixirs. Whenever he talked about it, she'd smile at him in the condescending way that older siblings have and say: "Maman told me that's just make-believe."

"No, Papa said it's true," Robbie would argue. He'd run off to their library to find the antique leather-bound history book that by now fell open to the right page. He'd point to the engraving of Pliny the Elder, the Roman author and philosopher. "He saw Cleopatra's book of fragrance formulas. He writes about it right here."

She hated to disillusion her brother, but it was important he understand that it was all just an exaggerated story. If she could convince him, then maybe she could believe it herself.

"There might have been an inventory of the perfumes Cleopatra's factory had manufactured, but we don't have it. And there's no such thing as the Fragrance of Memory. There can't be a perfume that makes you remember things. It's all a fairy tale our ancestors made up so that the House of L'Etoile would seem more exotic. For over two hundred years, our family has created and manufactured perfumes and sold them from our store. Just perfumes, Robbie. Mixtures of oils and alcohol. Not dreams. Not fantasies. Those are all made up, Robbie. To entertain us."

Her mother had taught her all about stories. The ones you made up on purpose. And the ones that came unbidden. "Even when they are frightening and hold you in their grip, you can control them," Audrey would say with a knowing look in her eye. Jac understood. Her mother was giving Jac clues. Helping her deal with what made the two of them different from the others.

Despite her mother's advice, make-believe had still nearly driven Jac insane. As bad as her visions had been when Audrey was alive, they intensified with her mother's death. And there had been no way Jac could convince herself they weren't real.

After months of doctors who prescribed treatments and drugs that not only didn't help but sometimes made her feel even crazier, one finally saw inside her and understood her. He taught her to distill the terrors the way perfumers took flowers and extracted their essences. Then he worked with her to make sense of all those droplets of screaming, bleeding hallucinations. He showed her how to find the symbolism in her delusions and to use mythological and spiritual archetypes to interpret them. Symbols, he explained, don't have to relate to a person's actual life. More often, they are part of the collective unconscious. Archetypes are a universal language. They were the clues Jac needed to decipher her torment.

In one of Jac's most horrific recurring delusions, she was trapped in a burning room high above an apocalyptic city. The fourth wall was all windows. Desperately, as the smoke threatened to overwhelm her, she tried to find a way to open the casements. If only she could get out, she knew she could use the great translucent wings strapped to her back to fly to safety.

Somewhere beyond the room, she could hear people—albeit impossible over the roar of the fire. She screamed for help. But no one came to her rescue. She was going to die.

With the doctor's help, Jac examined her unconscious and was able to identify threads of the myth of Daedalus and Icarus. An important difference—that proved to be the clue to understanding the significance of the dream—was that in her nightmare she was alone. Both her father and her mother had forsaken her. Even if Icarus ignored his father's advice, his father was there, offering it. But no one was warning Jac not to fly too close to the sun or to the sea. She was abandoned. Imprisoned. Doomed. Fated to burn to death.

Learning about archetypes and symbolic imagery was the first step in a long road that led her to writing *Mythfinders* and then to producing the cable television show. Instead of becoming a perfumer like her brother and her father and his father before him, Jac had become an explorer, tracing the origins of ancient myths. She brought myths to life so that she could bring them down to earth. Traveling from Athens to Rome to Alexandria, she sought out archaeological landmarks and historical records, searching for proof of the people and events that had grown into myths.

Jac wanted to help people understand that stories existed as metaphors, lessons and maps—but not as truths. Magic can be dangerous. Reality was empowering. There were no Minotaurs. No monsters. There were no unicorns or fairies or ghosts. There was a line between fact and fantasy. And as an adult, she never took her eyes off of it.

Except when she came here, each year, on the tenth of May, on the anniversary of her mother's death.

The light shifted. Jac knew it was the clouds moving, but the impression it created was that the angel was breathing. How lovely it would be to believe a stone angel could come to life. That there were heroes who never disappointed. That her mother really did speak to her from the grave.

Ah, but I do, came the whispered response to Jac's unspoken thought. *You know I do. I know how dangerous you think it is for you to believe me—but talk to me, sweetheart, it will help.*

Jac stood and began to unwrap the apple blossoms she'd brought. She never spoke to the specter. Her mother wasn't actually here. The manifestation was caused by an abnormality in her brain. She'd seen the MRI on her father's desk and read the doctor's letter.

Jac was fourteen at the time—but she'd have to look up some of the words in the dictionary even now. The scan showed what they called a very slight reduction of volume in frontal white matter, the area where evidence of psychotic disease was sometimes found. Proof it wasn't her overactive imagination that made her feel as if she was going crazy but an abnormality doctors could see.

Although, it wasn't one they could treat with any certainty. The patient's long-term prognosis was uncertain. The condition might never become more pronounced than it was already. Or she could develop more severe bipolar tendencies.

The doctor recommended immediate therapy along with a cycle of psychopharmaceuticals to see if it relieved Jac's symptoms.

Jac tore off the cellophane packaging and crumpled it, the crackling loud but not loud enough to drown out her mother's voice.

I know this is upsetting for you, sweetheart, and I am sorry.

Once the branches were nestled in the urn under the stained-glass window on the west wall, they began to scent the air. Jac usually preferred shadowy, woodsy scents. Sharp spices and musk. Moss and pepper with only a hint of rose. But this sweet-smelling flower was her mother's favorite, and so she brought it year after year and let it remind her of all that she missed.

The sky darkened, and a sudden rainstorm beat against the glass. Crouching in front of the urn, Jac sat on her heels and listened to the drops hitting hard on the roof and pounding the windows. Usually she was impatient to get to the next appointment. To change the scenery. Not to linger. Anything to avoid the boredom that invited excess contemplation of the wrong kind. But here, in this crypt, once a year, Jac felt a kind of sick relief in giving in to her fear, grief and disillusionment. Here, in this abyss, in the sad blue light, she could just be still and care too much instead of not at all. She could allow herself the visions. Be frightened by them but not fight them. Just once a year. Just here.

When I was a little girl, I used to believe this light was a bridge that let me walk from the living to the dead and back again.

Jac could almost feel her mother stroking her hair as she spoke in that soft whisper she'd used when putting her to bed. Jac shut her eyes. The sound of the storm filled the silence until Audrey spoke again.

That's what it is for us, isn't it, sweetheart? A bridge?

Jac didn't speak. Couldn't. She listened for her mother's next words but instead heard the rain and then the whine of hinges as the heavy wrought-iron and glass door opened. She turned as a gust of wet cold wind blew in. Jac saw the shadow of a man and for a moment wasn't sure if that was real, either.

The story continues in *The Book of Lost Fragrances*, available in hardcover and eBook from **ATRIA** BOOKS.

COMING SOON FROM GILLIAN ROYES

The Man Who Turned Both Cheeks (December 2012)

THE GOAT WOMAN OF LARGO BAY

by *Gillian Royes*

Introducing Shadrack "Shad" Myers

Shadrack Myers is a charming quick-witted bartender and jack-of-all-trades for his village on the eastern end of Jamaica. Shad makes his living as the right hand of Eric, an American who has cast his lot with the citizens of Largo Bay. He loves to be in the middle of everything and sees himself as the local sheriff. Barely able to read and write, he has an abundance of common sense, compassion, and street smarts, and uses them to solve problems and keep the peace among locals and visitors in this remote island resort where all is not always well in paradise.

Read on for the first chapter of Gillian Royes's *The Goat Woman of Largo Bay* where you first meet Shad who observes offshore what seems to be a goat.

Currently available as a paperback and eBook from **ATRIA** BOOKS

Excerpt from
*The Goat Woman
of Largo Bay* © 2011
by Gillian Royes

Jamaica

At first he thought she was a goat. Staring at the distant spot, Shad decided there was something about goats that had always irritated him. Nobody liked them, even if they were as common to Largo as fishing boats. But they were rude animals—*facety*, his grandmother used to call them—invading your yard to eat your young tomatoes and glaring when you tried to shoo them away.

The thought came only a minute after Eric had shouted his name and Shad had placed the glass he'd been wiping on a shelf and hurried around the counter of the bar.

"What happening, boss?" he'd said.

"There's something on the island!" Eric, his T-shirt and shorts flattened by the sea breeze, was pointing toward the tiny offshore island.

"I don't see nothing." Shad had squinted at the lump of rocks and its lone tree. "Probably just a bird, or a shadow."

"I'm telling you, there's something out there."

A tall man with the red-brown skin of a northerner who'd been in the tropics too long, Eric was standing statue-still, knees bent, a few feet from the edge of the cliff. Every part of him, the outstretched arm holding a pipe, the swirling white hair, the small paunch even, strained toward the island.

Atop the five steps leading down to the grass, Shad had shielded his eyes against the setting sun. Golden-orange, the island looked like a prodigal son sitting a quarter mile offshore. The water that separated it from the cliff was striped turquoise and aqua, long waves rolling toward the shore, forever restless without a protective reef.

"I see it," Shad said.

"I told you so," Eric said, and straightened. "What do you think it is?"

"Look like a goat, boss."

Eric agreed, because Shadrack Myers was known in Largo Bay as a *smart-man*, in the best sense of the term. He might be small and wiry, they said, but he was as bright as any Kingston professor and as wily as Anansi, the spider of the folk tales. The reason for this, according to the old ladies, was that he was born with a high forehead and the blackest skin a man could have.

"Who'd put a damn goat out there?" Eric asked.

"It only take one renegade to cause confusion," Shad said. And the renegade knew that Eric wouldn't do anything, because a foreign man couldn't afford to make a fuss in a small Jamaican village.

"Why would they want to do that?" Eric said, and put his hands on his hips.

"Probably to separate it from the herd. Must be sick."

"Sick? They can't just take a sick goat out and leave it. Don't they know the place is mine?" Eric said, and raised his arms to heaven just as Shad turned away.

Few people other than Eric noticed the little island anymore, and Shad tried to see it the way his neighbors did, as nothing more than background wallpaper, like the tall mountains behind the village. Looking at the roofless, paint-stripped walls on the island only left a sweet-and-sour feeling in his stomach.

Behind the counter, Shad cut limes into thin slices and prodded the last of the cherries out of the bottle, wondering how to find the owner of the goat. If he started talking about the animal, someone might row out and steal the goat. But if he and Eric didn't do something, the owner might take other goats over, and there'd be even more trouble.

Setting a bottle of wine on the counter, he called to Eric.

"Boss, remember to order more red wine. We running low."

If any customers had been seated in the bar, they would never have known that the slim, midthirties man bustling behind the counter—the shirt neatly tucked into the belted pants—was thinking of anything other than the job at hand. Instead, and as foreigners sipping a beer often did, they would have thought that Shad was the happiest man in Jamaica—and missed the haunted look behind his eyes. They could have been forgiven, because it was easy to assume from his trademark grin, with its gap between the front teeth, that Shad was a man with few problems and a good ear; in other words, the perfect bartender.

While the bar was prepared for evening business, Eric sat on the top step, his back to Shad. The only response the younger man heard was a grunt, accompanied by a cloud of pipe tobacco, as always Canadian maple, which blew in with the sea breeze, filling the empty restaurant.

When it was finally too dark to see, Eric stood and tapped the dead ashes from his pipe bowl against the step. As he plodded past the bar, it was clear to Shad that the goat's invasion was hanging over them both. It had brought back regrets that would linger until they took action.

The next morning dawned drizzly and gray, unusual for Largo in midsummer. Visibility was poor and Shad spent most of the morning placing and emptying buckets under the bar's leaky thatch roof. Near him, Eric, his forehead lined with debt, sat at a wooden table in the bar calculating the cost of a new roof, looking up from his paperwork a few times to ask the name of a workman or a hardware store, glancing at the island while he did it.

"Boss," Shad finally asked, his voice offhanded, "you going out to the island?"

"Nah, I don't think so," Eric said. He looked up and rubbed his knees, the way he did when it rained. "Did you find out who took a goat out? Anyone with a sick goat?"

"Half the goats around here are sick, man," Shad said, rubbing a hand over his shaved head. Speculation in front of Eric was never a good idea, because next thing, he'd be driving all over town asking questions and making accusations.

Two days later, pushing in and straightening chairs after lunch, a broom in one hand, Shad glanced up and saw someone rowing toward the island. The bright purple and red canoe was carved from a single log, like most of the older fishing boats. It beached on the eastern side of the island. The rower offloaded a few bags and disappeared. Staring without blinking, feeling behind him to make sure he didn't miss the chair, Shad sat and watched the person return, again with bags, and row back east around the point.

A goat, a man rowing bags of things to and from the island—they didn't add up to Shad, and he knew everything that went on in Largo. In a community of five hundred in an isolated corner of Jamaica, a village without a police station or a hospital, someone had to make it their job to sniff out—and snuff out—problems even before they emerged, and Shad was that man.

The bartender's vocation as sniffer and snuffer had started in early childhood because he was a fierce runner, and since he was also a nice child, his ability to run had earned him many a ten-cents. When the nurse in the clinic was needed, when money had to be paid to the *obeah man*, the magician on the hill, it was Shad they called. And every night, when he lay next to his grandmother in her iron bed, she snoring so loudly he could hardly fall asleep, he would think about what errand he'd run that day and what problem he'd helped to solve. And decades later he would do the same, lying beside a sleeping Beth, thinking about the woman, the woman he'd thought was a goat.

The purple and red boat remained a puzzle to Shad even after a few discreet inquiries. Avoiding the fish market, where they gossiped too much for an investigation this subtle in nature, he questioned a few older fishermen who hung around the bar at night. But for all the complimentary white rums he provided, no one knew of the boat or a separated goat. It was just enough to intrigue a man who had to know.

———————

The story continues in *The Goat Woman of Largo Bay,* available in paperback and eBook from **ATRIA** BOOKS.

ALSO BY A. D. SCOTT

A Small Death in the Great Glen

A DOUBLE DEATH ON THE BLACK ISLE

by A. D. Scott

Introducing Joanne Ross

She's a mother of two young girls, a typist and budding reporter at a local newspaper . . . and a battered wife. In the Scottish Highlands in the late 1950s, Joanne Ross is a woman ahead of her time: she found the strength to find a job and leave her abusive, war-scarred husband. And though the scorn of the community—including her own in-laws—is frequently heaped upon her, the murders of her life-long friend's husband and a local worker prove to be even more difficult to handle . . .

———————

The excerpt that follows introduces you to *A Double Death in the Black Isle*'s Joanne Ross, giving you a glimpse into the complicated world in which she lives.

Currently available as a paperback and eBook from **ATRIA** BOOKS

Scotland

Excerpt from
*A Double Death on
the Black Isle* © 2011
by A. D. Scott

The bruising on Joanne Ross was invisible. Like a peach with the flesh discolored around the stone, she seemed untouched. But the shame of "having to get married," that understated euphemism for the rush to the altar, followed by a six-month pregnancy, marred her own marriage and caused her parents to disown her. Ten years on, they had not relented; they had never forgiven her for shaming them, never met their grandchildren. The pain has softened but when asked by friends, by her children, she made excuses about never visiting—the price of the train tickets, her parents being too elderly to have young children around, anything other than tell the truth.

She was aware that she was a quarter-step ahead or behind the beat of the community. Her mood often depended on the weather, her opinions seemingly influenced by a mischievous imp hovering somewhere in the region of her left shoulder. A tune, a song, a poem could change her walk. Her wide-open face showed the bloodlines of a true Scot. But her cheekbones were on the edge of too strong, her mouth on the side of too wide, and her skin too freckled to be considered beautiful.

She knew her husband was ashamed of her; he'd married a woman who would never fit in, in the Highland town where respectability was all-important and being "different" was a sin.

"Stubborn," her husband, Bill Ross, called her. "Too much schooling" in her mother-in-law's opinion. "Stuck up" was the phrase one of the mothers at the school had used. *A mind of her own*, McAllister thought, but he meant that as praise.

Joanne shook off thoughts of her failed marriage and went back to typing. She worked steadily, her athletic shoulders wrestling with the heavy, awkward typewriter as easily as a cowboy with a steer, plowing through lists scribbled on scrap paper, typed notes, scrawls on the back of an envelope, and one that just said "repeat last year's." They were all notices of the holidays and events surrounding Easter.

She glanced at the clock, one surely stolen from a railway station waiting room, and noted she had five minutes before anyone else would appear. She made tidy piles of the bits of copy paper, the finished work ready for Don's pencil. Then she would retype it all over again. How she could continue with all this, plus her new job as full-time reporter and her new status as a single mother, she hadn't yet worked out.

Ask for help, Rob had suggested. But she couldn't. Not wouldn't, couldn't. Silly I know, she told herself often, recognizing in herself that trait that seemed to be one of mothers and women in general, that catchall phrase used when help was offered—I can manage. Yes, she could manage, but only by being first in, last out.

"Blast," Joanne spoke out loud. "Five minutes more, that's all I need." The phone kept ringing. "Double blast." It wasn't going to stop. "*Highland Gazette.*" She sighed.

"Just the girl I'm after."

"Patricia Ord Mackenzie—you are psychic. I was about to call you." A small white lie—Joanne *had* been meaning to call Patricia, but first she needed to don an armor-plated carapace of confidence to deal with her oldest friend.

"It's all that water from the Fairy Well I've been downing—makes me psychic," Patricia laughed.

"We're looking forward to this Easter holiday." Joanne meant it. Holidays away were not something she could afford, but she was looking forward to a few days away—as long as they didn't have to spend much time with Patricia's mother.

"The girls are driving me crazy with questions about the Black Isle. Are your parents prepared for the onslaught of two lively children?"

Patricia laughed again.

"The house is big. We can avoid them as much as possible."

Joanne wholeheartedly agreed with her friend. As much space as possible between her, her children, and Patricia's mother would be a very good idea. The Ord Mackenzie family was very grand in an estate-owning, ancient-name, Highland-gentry way. And Mrs. Janet Ord Mackenzie made certain that everyone showed due deference to her as the lady of the estate.

"Anyway," Patricia continued, "I've called to ask you to come early. The eight-o'clock ferry. I've something special planned."

"Eight on a Thursday? It'll mean a rush. Everyone at the *Gazette* usually goes out together on Wednesday night, and this week is special as we're . . ."

"I'll pick you up at the jetty and we'll go straight there."

"Go where?" Joanne was intrigued.

"A surprise. I've some really good news."

"So have I. We're launching the new *Gazette*, and I've been given the front page, my first big story. It's really exciting, it's about a fire and . . ."

"Wear your glad rags tomorrow," Patricia interrupted. "It's a special day."

"Now you've got me really curious." She caved in—as Patricia knew she would. "Fine then. Eight-o'clock ferry."

Joanne hung up the telephone. "Patricia Ord Mackenzie," she muttered, "what are you up to?"

Feeling slighted, she looked up at the ceiling, and shaking her head, said, "Thanks for listening to me too, Patricia. Thanks for being interested in *my* life."

Although they had met when they were seven, and had been at boarding school together for the whole of their education, Joanne was never sure if they were close—there was a touch of the bully in her friend. Perhaps it was their family circumstances. Patricia came from a wealthy, landowning family; Joanne was a daughter of the manse. But, Joanne acknowledged, in their years in a bleak, Scottish boarding school, where crying singled you out as a baby, they had formed an unlikely friendship, a friendship of girls who never quite fitted in with the clique. Or at least Joanne assumed it was a friendship. *So why do I always feel inferior when I am with Patricia? Why do I always give in?*

The noise on the stone stairway interrupted Joanne's reverie. Everyone seemed to materialize in the reporters' room at the same time—a difficult feat given the width of the stairs.

"I declare the news conference open. All aboard and correct and ready for D-Day?" McAllister looked around the ensemble, taking in the nods and grins and ayes and the shrug from Don. "Mrs. Smart?"

"I'm pleased with the response from our advertisers, Mr. McAllister. Most have taken more space. There is also a full page from Arnotts advertising the latest televisions."

"Well done, Mrs. Smart. Don?"

"The printers and compositors are ready." He didn't mention he'd promised them a bonus of a couple of bottles of whisky if they got the new edition out on time. "The expanded sports pages are looking good," he continued, "Countryside column too. The only problem with it is the length of Mr. Mortimer Beauchamp Carlyle's name. Maybe we should give him a pseudonym. . . ."

"Five shillings for the best suggestion," McAllister declared. "On the subject of new columns, I'm instituting one, the title is

'For a' That'. It will go on the opinion page, I'll use it to stir things up a bit."

"Only if it is checked by a legal eagle," Don told him.

"Naturally. Rob?" McAllister asked.

"I've a report on the plans for the new bridge across the river. I did a vox pop as you suggested. A surprising number of people are concerned that another bridge would fulfill the Brahan Seer's prophecy and bring disaster to the town."

"Don," McAllister turned to him, "a heading stating a threat to the town from a seventeenth-century seer would be great. Joanne?"

"I've written up the fire and covered the meeting with the fire chief. I think that's everything."

"I see." He was busy and brusque and wanted Joanne to stop looking nervous every time he asked her a question. "Did you call the fire chief for an update? The police? The procurator fiscal's office to ask what the charge will be? Do you have a quote from anyone in the fishing village in the Black Isle? This must be a big event for them. The west coast connection, what's that about? Have anything to add to turn this into a front page to remember?"

McAllister hadn't noticed Joanne getting pinker and pinker and squirming on her stool as he counted off the phone calls yet to be made, facts yet to be ascertained, opinions yet to be canvassed. But Don did.

"For heaven's sake, give the lassie time to draw breath." Don pointed his finger at Rob. "You, you talk to the polis seeing as how you're so pally with Woman Police Constable McPherson. You, McAllister, call your new pal Beauchamp in the Black Isle; see if he's heard any gossip. Me, I'll talk to my contact in the procurator fiscal's office *and* I'll call our man on the west coast, see if he can find out anything, and Joanne," he turned to her, "call the fire chief, ask if he's finished his report and ask if you can have a sneak look at it. Use your charms. Then, let's say . . ." he glanced at the clock, ". . . eleven thirty, we'll get together and see where we're at."

"Yes, Mr. McLeod." Rob laughed.

"And you," he pointed to his boss, "in your office now, I'd like a wee word."

Don carefully shut the door of McAllister's office, well aware that Rob and Joanne would be waiting to hear the explosion. But he wasn't going to give them the satisfaction.

McAllister sat down, lit a cigarette, and waited for Don to do the same.

"This fire is a big story," Don started. "It's not every day you hear about Molotov cocktails in the Highlands. It's a great front page to launch the paper." Don's tone changed to a low, pre-bark growl. "But for heaven's sake, just because you fancy the lassie and are getting nowhere, stop taking your frustration out on her. I'm not having it. Right?"

Don left, closing the door behind him before McAllister could recover enough to reply.

The meeting later in the morning to pull together the story of the firebombing was productive. Joanne had written five hundred words from the point of view of the firemen. She also had a brief account from a neighbor who had been waiting in her car to cross the canal when the fire broke out.

"Good lively stuff, Joanne," Don commented as he took his wee red pencil to the more extravagant quotes.

Don read through Rob's report on the comments from the police. "The usual 'Saw nothing, heard nothing, know nothing,'"

Don called it. "The procurator fiscal's office would only say 'The accident inquiry is in progress,'" Don added, "so not much there."

"No, but this story is looking good. It has legs." McAllister was happy. "One, we have a great picture," he started, counting off the points with his fingers.

"Don't tell Hec that, or we'll never hear the end of it." Rob was still smarting at Hec being made a full-time member of the team.

"Two, this is a good description of the fire, Joanne—colorful but succinct." McAllister went on, "I like the interview you did with the firemen—you got the balance between the facts and the human interest just right; your interview with the witness who saw it all from the beginning is sharp and newsworthy."

"I had trouble getting off the phone, the woman blethered so much." Joanne smiled and blushed at the praise.

"Three, the whole mystery as to why the boat was making its way to the west coast rather than home. Graham Nicolson, our stringer in Fort William, will investigate. That should give us something for the next edition."

"I think this story will run for at least a couple more editions," Rob interrupted. "The police are completely baffled as to why anyone would firebomb a fishing boat. They have no suspects, no clues."

"'Police Baffled.'" Don was delighted. "A favorite headline of we hacks in the newspaper trade."

McAllister rolled his eyes and held up his hand again. "Finally, Beech has heard rumors of a family feud involving the owner of the boat."

"I like it," Don agreed. "Family feuds—great copy. But keep that for the next edition."

"All right, let's put this together, we only have five hours."
McAllister paused, "Joanne, everyone, thanks—good work."

Mondays, news meeting; Tuesdays, two days to finish the
paper—the routine was busy, but steady busy. Now it was
Wednesday, and Wednesdays were for panic, a noisy late
afternoon panic, but controlled like the panic of sailing—quiet
stretches, then a burst of weather to keep everyone on their toes.

This Wednesday, with the deadline for the new *Gazette*
looming, tension came early to the reporters' room. It had an
almost visible presence. The dust motes, in a beam through
the north-facing window, seemed thicker than usual. The low,
churning, industrial noises of the presses in the bowels of the
building had started earlier than usual. Even the typewriters
seemed heavier.

Joanne and Rob were attempting to type in quick time
instead of waltz time, so the machines jammed more often, the
paper disappearing into the jaws of the monsters. A carriage
stuck. A ribbon unwound. Sometimes this happened at the
same time. Joanne spoke sternly to the Underwood with ladylike
expletives. Rob thumped his.

Don moved up and down the three flights of stairs to the
presses more briskly. McAllister popped in more often, asking
more questions.

Five o'clock, the tempo accelerated to real time. Don was to
and from the reporters and the typesetters, bringing copy, waiting
at the stone, signing off on pages. McAllister, his jobs done, was
hovering around like an expectant father outside the maternity
ward, getting in everyone's way.

At six o'clock, Don returned with some finished pages.

"They look good, no, they're great," pronounced McAllister.

Rob and Joanne leaned back from their machines, their part of the process finished at last. Simultaneously they stretched their arms out, glanced at each other, and grinned.

Rob looked around the room. "Station Hotel?" he asked. It was the only safe place to take Joanne; her reputation would be seriously besmirched should she be seen in a public bar.

"You two go," McAllister said. "Don and I still have a lot to do."

"Sorry Rob, I need an early night." Joanne regretted her promise to Patricia; she would have loved to stay with the others. "I'm off to the Black Isle for Easter and have to catch an early ferry tomorrow morning."

Rob decided to stay on at the *Gazette* office. The excitement of waiting for the first pages was infectious.

Eight thirty—another hour, maybe less, and the first edition of the new *Highland Gazette*, Easter 1957, would be printed. This is history, McAllister realized, the first real change in a hundred years.

The abiding fear of an editor of a small-town newspaper was to print an article, a headline, destined to become one of the notorious legends of newspaper lore, one of the stories relayed to journalism cadets in every newspaper in the country. He remembered one apocryphal story. An Aberdeen paper, the day the Second World War was declared, ran a front page devoted to the local Agricultural show—"Local Man Wins Prize for Biggest Turnip," or did they say neap? He wasn't quite sure.

Eight o'clock came, and he couldn't wait any longer. Walking downstairs, he cheered immensely. This was the sound and the smell of a newspaper. Normally Don, the father of the chapel, and the comps would chase everyone, even the editor, out of the hallowed ground of the stone.

But tonight was different. The comps and printers nodded silently as McAllister joined them, understanding his need to be there. The noise from the press, the clanking, the whirring, the steady industrial hum, filled the basement. The very walls, carved from solid stone, seemed to vibrate.

Rob joined them, hovering by the big machine, mesmerized by the cogs and flywheels and conveyor belts all awhirl, clanking out copies of the broadsheet pages before they went shooting off to be sorted and folded into a tabloid format, then shunted to a man who would stack them and tie them into neat bundles of newspaper.

Forty-five minutes later, the first copies rolled off the press. Don had already reviewed individual pages, but this was the first neatly folded copy of the newspaper, ink fresh and barely dry. A printer lifted one from the growing pile and ceremonially handed it to McAllister. McAllister grinned. They shook hands.

Don grinned as his copy was handed to him. Rob waved from across the shop floor and came to join them. There were more handshakes, a slap or two on various backs, the father of the chapel and the printers joined in, grinning, before turning back to nurse the fickle machines.

Rob left. The roar of his motorbike echoed through the empty streets as he sped home to share the new *Highland Gazette* with his parents. He debated whether to take a copy to Joanne, but decided it was not the done thing to arrive late at night on a quiet suburban street at the house of a woman who had walked out on her marriage.

McAllister took two more copies, one to dissect, one as a souvenir. Don joined him on the steps of the *Gazette* building. They looked at each other.

"It's a start," came McAllister's verdict.

"Aye."

And the two men, who from a distance resembled a reverse Laurel and Hardy—the skinny one tall, the fat one short—strode off in opposite directions into the dark of the town, both trying vainly to keep a grin of satisfaction from breaking out, frequently.

———————

The story continues in *A Double Death on the Black Isle*, available in paperback and eBook from **ATRIA** BOOKS.

SOUTH BY SOUTHEAST

by Blair Underwood, Tananarive Due, and Steven Barnes

Introducing Tennyson Hardwick

He's a gorgeous but failing actor and stuntman living on the fringes of the good life in Hollywood, always hoping for the ever-elusive big break. In the past, when times got tough, Tennyson fell into the shadow world of male escorts, a high-paid gigolo for moneyed women from every corner of society. Now, he's struggling to redeem himself—especially in the eyes of his father, a pioneering, decorated LAPD captain. Tennyson discovers his hidden talent as a sleuth when he has to save himself from taking the fall for the murder of a female rapper.

———————

Read on for the first chapter of *South by Southeast* where Tennyson gets personal sharing his thoughts on those closest to him—his dad, on-again off-again girlfriend April, and adopted daughter, Chela.

Available as a paperback and eBook in September 2012 from **ATRIA** BOOKS

Excerpt from *South by Southeast* © 2012 by Trabajando, Inc., Tananarive Due, and Steven Barnes

Florida

Salsa is joy itself, but the pealing trumpets, precise piano, ticking clave, and rallying cowbell always make me sad. Salsa is the sound of Miami, and Miami . . .

Let's just say that Miami changed everything. Forever.

Salsa was blaring the night of Marcela's birthday, when I was showing off the fruits of the dance lessons that had once been a part of my trade. Dancing comes easily to me, so I was delighting Marcela's sisters and girlfriends by twirling them two at a time—one in front, one in back—spinning and weaving through the intricate beat like a black Fred Astaire. Anybody watching me would have thought I'd been raised in the heart of Havana or San Juan. *¡Baile!*

I hate to brag, but this brother can dance his ass off in any language.

That night, my life's pieces were still in place. When I have trouble sleeping, I hold that snapshot in my head, every detail crisp as life. Close enough to touch. My patio was packed with Marcela Ruiz's relatives, aunts and cousins and siblings of all ages and sizes dancing with equal fervor. I didn't know anyone at the party. I didn't even have a date.

Marcela was my father's girlfriend, although "girlfriend" is a funny word for a woman in her fifties whose "boyfriend" is pushing eighty. Marcela brought my father back from the dead. She had become his special friend when he had his stroke and ended up in a nursing home years before. Marcela was an RN, and she'd taken a liking to Dad before he could speak or move, appreciating what was left. At the time, I couldn't see anything left of Dad myself. Marcela gave me my father back. LAPD Captain Richard Allen Hardwick (Ret.) was a pretty cool guy.

Dad and I were doing better the second time around. I felt a slow tension coiling with each passing month, a part of me bracing for the next time Dad would go to a hospital. I'd believed he was as good as gone at the nursing home, and I'd never been so wrong about anything. When the time came, it would be the worst day of my life. I could tell already.

Dad couldn't dance the way he used to—he could barely walk—but he was dressed for the dance floor in white linen slacks and matching guayabera. He bobbed his head to the salsa beat, walking with the polished wooden Ethiopian cane my ex had given him as a gift. Dad worked his cane like a fashion statement. He had made peace with his limitations somehow.

When I doubted miracles, I remembered Dad rising from his body's ashes.

Dad hovered over his party like a movie director. "Hey!" he barked at a middle-aged man wearing black. "Get that damn pig away from the dance floor."

A wide-hipped woman turned over her shoulder, shooting him a nasty look. While her hips rocked with exuberant worship to Rubén Blades, she'd nearly sent the serving cart and its whole roasted *cerdo* flying to the floor. The pig was a traditional Cuban meal Dad had ordered for Marcela, and the skewer rammed through the porcine mouth, emerging on the other end, was enough to make me want to swear off pork. Dad had ordered enough food to feed a village.

"Do you speak *inglés*?" Dad said, raising his voice. "Move it, *por favor*."

Great. After two years of speech therapy, unfortunately, people could understand almost everything Dad said. Marcela's cousin Fernando, a neurosurgeon from West Palm Beach I'd introduced to Dad an hour before, didn't appreciate being mistaken for the help. He stared at Dad with a combination of pity and loathing.

I gently led Dad away from Marcela's cousin. "Sorry, man," I whispered to Fernando. "You know how it is."

"No," Fernando said, and sipped from his mojito. "I don't know how it is. In fact, I'd very much like to understand, but . . ." He shrugged, leaving the thought hanging.

Like everyone in Marcela's family, he wondered why she was wasting her last hunting years with an old man on a cop's pension. Dad was old enough to be Marcela's father too. If I weren't so confused about it myself, Fernando's attitude might have pissed me off. Dad was seventy-six, and he didn't even have charm on his side.

"El corazón quiere lo que quiere," I said, repeating the phrase Marcela had spoken when I'd finally gotten up the nerve to ask her The Question. "The heart wants what it wants."

Fernando huffed a curse in Spanish and moved away, tired of conversation. I couldn't blame him. That single phrase had justified endless reckless behavior and heartaches. A copout. Maybe Marcela had daddy issues. Maybe she had a fetish for wrinkles. Maybe she only felt safe when she was in control. Or maybe . . .

Or hell, maybe she was in love with him. I tried to count Dad's good qualities from Marcela's point-of-view: He stayed home, never running the streets. He didn't talk much so he was a good listener. And he threw a hell of a birthday party, apparently—even if the best he'd done for me was bringing cupcakes to my elementary school's day care.

Dad had created a Cubana's wonderland for Marcela, with

white Christmas lights strung across my South Beach condo's patio and balcony like stars hanging above the beachfront. A feast had been catered by her favorite restaurant, with roast pig, black beans and rice, fried plantains, and fried yucca. A five-member salsa band was working the crowd of fifty into a sweat. Dad had even sprung for a butterfly-shaped ice sculpture, although the painstaking creation wasn't faring well in the warm, humid fall night.

Marcela had been slimming down for the trip to Miami for weeks, so she'd squeezed into a short silver glitter dress that was snug in all the right places and showed off the hard-won definition in her smooth calves, the fruit of her new morning jogging regimen. Marcela Ruiz had seemed plain when I met her, but she had blossomed under my father's care. Dad stared at her as if she were perfection itself.

But what happens in five years? Or one or two? Six months? I didn't like those thoughts, but it was hard to avoid them when Dad's prescription bottles could fill a Hefty bag. Nothing in his body worked without jumper cables. Marcela understood that better than anyone.

"How much did all this cost, anyway?" I asked Dad, teasing him. Until he'd met Marcela, he'd been the most frugal man I'd ever known. Even my fifth-grade cupcakes had been two days past fresh, on sale.

"None of your business," Dad said. He looked nervous, fumbling in the pocket of his slacks as if he'd misplaced something. A medicine bottle? He took nitroglycerine tablets for his painful angina, which mimicked heart attack symptoms. Perspiration beaded his dark forehead.

"You all right, Dad?"

His least favorite question. "I'm not a damn child," Dad said. He nearly tripped over his feet as he pivoted away from the catering table, but I didn't move to steady him. Our dance.

I wandered to the balcony with my bottle of Red Stripe and stared out at Ocean Drive's collection of Art Deco hotels lit up in candy shop neon. I'd spent too much money renting the two-bedroom suite for my shoot, even at the "friend" price from a woman I knew who'd made a fortune when South Beach flipped from Retirement City to Vacation Haven in the nineties, but what the hell? My family was celebrating my casting in a horror film like they thought I was headed for the A list. Chela, the teenager I'd rescued from my former madam, had graduated from high school and would be going to college . . . eventually. We were taking our first family vacation—maybe our first and last. I wanted it to count. I had money sitting in my bank account after winning a sexual harassment settlement against producer powerhouse Lynda Jewell. Long story, and it was far behind me.

Neon. South Beach. The salty-sweet ocean air. Perfecto.

Beyond the neon's glare, my beachfront perch was close enough for me to make out the moonlit Atlantic, as still as a sheet of black glass. Pinpricks of lights from distant cruise ships or cargo vessels twinkled in the distance, but the water was undisturbed.

Even on the hottest summer days, SoCal's ocean seems immune from the sun. Now it was fall, and I went swimming practically every day, often after dark, when the beaches emptied. Heaven. I didn't need a ride; a calm, warm bath felt just fine.

Watching the ocean made me think of my ex, April. I almost reached for my cell phone, until I remembered that April was still at work for another hour on the West Coast. I felt itchy if I didn't talk to her every night. How had I let myself end up in a long-distance relationship? Only you're not in a relationship anymore—remember?

One day, April and I would have to put a name to what we had. Friends Extra? Lovers Lite? We'd collected enough pain over four years to make us both wary of labels, but we couldn't keep hiding from each other forever. *You're the one who's hiding,* I corrected myself. We both knew the next move was up to me. If April nudged me and I pulled back, we would never have another chance to salvage whatever we were trying to build.

"Isn't true love beautiful?" Chela said, startling me from behind. I thought she'd taken up mind-reading, until I saw her gazing toward Dad and Marcela. They both stood close to the dead pig, swaying gently to the band's bolero. Dad wobbled, but he didn't fall.

Chela had just turned eighteen, nearly as tall as I was, with a lithe model's figure, a scalp full of wild corkscrew ringlets and a sun-browned complexion that kept observers guessing about her ethnicity. In Miami, most people assumed she was Cuban. Modeling scouts had approached Chela as she strolled South Beach's streets with me, but so far I'd managed to talk her out of taking any meetings. I'd argued that the scouts weren't from Elite or Ford, so why settle for anything less than the best? In truth, as a college dropout who'd left school to pursue acting, I knew that if she put school off to do modeling shoots, she would never bother to go.

But I felt guilty discouraging her. She wasn't avoiding the scouts because of any advice from me; she just didn't see the same beautiful face in the mirror the scouts did. Chela was slowly emerging from her cocoon of drab, bulky clothes where she'd been hiding. Ocean Drive Chela wore bikinis and sheer fabrics, but not the Chela I knew at home.

"So, what's true love?" Sometimes the girl dropped wisdom.

"You're asking me?" Chela said. "Please."

"You're the one who said it."

Chela shrugged. Instead of looking at me, she stared toward the ocean. "Loving someone no matter how scary it is," she said. "No matter what anybody says or thinks."

After Chela's adolescent liaisons with johns twice her age, her definition of true love could excuse almost any toxic behavior. I used to live by the same credo, and my old life had nothing to do with love.

"Not good enough for you?" Chela said.

"Maybe," I said, noncommittal.

Chela gave me a cutting look. "You're the one who asked. Not my fault if you can't deal with the answer."

She started to walk away, but stopped in her tracks when Dad rang his martini glass with a knife. The patio slowly hushed except for the slow-moving traffic on Ocean Drive below us; laughter, bicycle bells, and revving motors.

Chela grabbed my arm, excited. "It's time," she whispered to me, grinning.

Once again, I was the last to hear almost everything under my roof. I'd been invisible to Dad when I was Chela's age, and she was his new best buddy. Call me childish, but I felt a sting of annoyance.

Then I was captivated by the sound of Dad's voice; he spoke slowly, careful to enunciate, all evidence of his stroke gone as he rediscovered his basso voice that had made him a coveted public speaker. "Marcela's the birthday girl today, but I'm hoping she'll be gracious enough to give me the gift of a lifetime," he said.

Dad sounded like himself again for the first time in years. Dad suddenly clasped Marcela's hands and stared into her eyes. I knew what was coming, and I doubted the night's fairy tale would have a happy ending.

"Marcela Maria Ruiz . . . ," Dad said, "will you marry me?"

The gasps that followed were more shock than delight. I think I gasped too, at least to myself. The night froze. Marcela's face was slack. When I'd once joked to Marcela that she would be my Evil Stepmother one day, she'd looked me dead in the eye and said, "I'm a romantic, Tennyson, but I'm also a realist."

Chela grinned widely enough to make up for the stunned paralysis from the rest of us.

She grabbed my elbow, clinging tightly, as if we riding a roller-coaster together.

Marcela blinked, and her eyes pooled with tears. She looked confused. "Captain?"

That was what she called my father—Captain Hardwick. At first, the formality had seemed like a ruse to hide their relationship, but the pet name had stuck. It was only one of the unconventional aspects of their union.

Dad reached into his pocket and brought out a felt ring case. After a couple of tries, he flipped it open: my inheritance sparkled inside. The ring was big enough to see from a distance. Marcela gaped at the engagement ring, her face flaring bright red.

"I know . . . it's a surprise," Dad said, more quietly this time. If not for the patio's hush, I wouldn't have heard him. But we spectators didn't want to miss a word. A woman close to me was tossing yucca fries into her mouth like popcorn as she watched.

This conversation was none of our business.

"Dios mio," Marcela said, flustered. She hid half her face with her hand, as if to shield herself from the crowd. Marcela's voice trembled. "You said . . ."

"I know what I said," Dad cut her off. "What you said. What . . . we said. Let sleeping dogs lie. Face facts. No need to be . . . foolish."

For the first time, he hesitated as if he were struggling for words, either because of emotion or his lingering disability. "But I was still hanging on to . . . the past. When I buried Eva, I swore I'd never . . . take another wife."

Marcela blinked, and a single tear made a snail's slow journey across her cheek.

"It's time, Marcy," Dad said. "If not now . . . when? I can't promise you . . . forever. But I can promise to love you every day. And I'll do whatever . . . it takes . . . to stay by your side as many years as I can."

Dad looked exhausted, his last words mere breath. Beside him, Marcela seemed younger and more vibrant than ever; the sun shining beside a fading star. She shook her head back and forth, almost imperceptibly, maybe a reflex. Damn. My mother had died when I was a baby, and I'd never known Dad to be interested in any woman before Marcela. When had he ever taken a woman out, except to a meeting? Stubborn fool! Why had he waited until it was too—

"Yes!" Marcela said, wrapping her arms around Dad. When Dad swayed beneath her weight, she steadied him. "I'll marry you. It is my honor, Captain Hardwick!"

More gasps came, louder than before. Chela applauded loudly, and I shook myself from my shock to join her clapping. A few other people clapped too, but I think they were the caterers and maybe the scattered children, who loved any excuse to make loud noises.

Most of Marcela's family just stared, never waking from their stunned silence.

"Oh, that's just wrong," April said.

I laughed grimly. "Which part?"

I'd finally caught April for our nightly phone date at about eleven—eight o'clock California time—when she got back to her apartment after shopping at Whole Foods. I knew her routine, could practically see her opening her whitewashed kitchen cabinets and metallic fridge with her long pianist's fingers while she put her food away. She'd been a reporter for the *LA Times* when I met her, but since her layoff a year ago she was working publicity for an entertainment PR firm. Whenever I asked how work was going, she said she didn't want to talk about it. Her newshound's soul hadn't adjusted to babysitting celebrities, but the job market was tight.

I'd closed my bedroom door to mute the party noise from revelers who hadn't gotten the hint when Marcela and Dad went to bed at ten. The band had left and the food was gone, but Marcela's kin were determined to dance to the mix blaring from her nephew's speakers. The party had started at five in the afternoon, and some folks were still showing up—on Cuban Time, as Marcela had complained. No one group can claim exclusive rights to tardiness.

I would have a hell of a mess to clean up in the morning, but morning was a world away and I was alone with April's voice. We'd tried keeping out of each other's way after she dumped me, but somehow we'd gotten tangled up again. Before the shoot, we'd been seeing each other two or three times a week, more than we had when we were officially dating.

April's laugh was music. "What kind of son are you?"

"You know I love Dad, but he's up there in age."

"It's not like they'll want to have kids."

I tried not to feel the prick. During a fateful dinner in Cape Town, April had given me a last chance to win her back, a Get Out of Jail Free card, and I'd blown it with my shock when she mentioned the idea of raising a family together. I'd practically raised a kid already, so why had I nearly choked on my food when April brought up wanting to have children?

Instinct made me change the subject fast. "What about a honeymoon?"

"What about it?" April said. "Don't you think you're confusing sex with intimacy? Besides, you don't know what they do behind closed doors."

A sour mixture of garlic and something tangy played at the base of my throat, and I had to work to flush away the image of Dad and Marcela in bed together. Besides, what had possessed me to bring up Dad's proposal? April never made it a secret when she had a date, and the sole reason we weren't officially together anymore was because April believed she was too old to have a "boyfriend" at nearly thirty. If I didn't ask her to marry me, I would lose her. It wasn't a threat; it was prophecy.

"Well, I think it's beautiful," April said primly.

"No, you're right—it was," I said. "I was just scared for him, thinking she would back off . . . but she didn't. She'll be with him until the end. What's more beautiful than that?"

Our silence stretched the length of Ocean Drive.

"Let me fly you down this weekend," I said. She'd been promising to visit the set.

"Can't," she said. "Award season. How do women walk in ten-foot shoes? I'm too much of a tomboy to wear dresses every night. I feel like a transvestite."

Good. Between the Golden Globes, the People's Choice Awards, the NAACP Image Award, and every honor until the Oscars, April wouldn't have much time to meet new men. Except the rich and famous ones, my Evil Voice reminded me.

"Cutest tomboy on stilettos I ever saw," I said. "Anyway, I'll make a visit worth your while. I can get you a sit-down with Gustavo."

April could always be lured closer with the right carrot, and my film's director, Gustavo Escobar, was the whole enchilada. April supplemented her publicity work with freelance journalism, and Escobar was a near-recluse who was impossible to reach when he was working on a project. An interview with him might be the coup she was looking for to help her land a job on the staff of *Entertainment Weekly*. Even if not, she might impress her bosses by convincing him to sign with her agency. April was looking for any break she could get.

Gustavo Escobar's enlistment to helm a horror movie was the fanboy coup of the year, evidence that horror and prestige weren't mutually exclusive. He'd won at Sundance and been nominated for a foreign-language Oscar for his last film, *Nuestro Tío Fidel*, which he'd shot guerrilla-style in his homeland of Cuba. Our current project, *Freaknik*, was more blood and guts than heart and soul, but he was a meticulous craftsman.

I wished my part were bigger, as always, but my agent thought it was the right move for me on the heels of art-house juggernaut *Lenox Avenue*, which had just been released to slobbering reviews. My slim part in *Lenox Avenue* had barely survived the editing booth, but it was still listed on my IMDB.com page for the film world to see.

Play your cards right, Ten, and this could be a new beginning for you, my agent had lectured me at our last lunch before I left for Miami. He knew I chased trouble like a junkie. A year ago, I'd been a household name for all the wrong reasons. Unless you live in a cave, you know about my brush with actress Sofia Maitlin. Even that wasn't enough for me. In the past six months, I'd allowed a bad influence in my life to get me in new trouble I hadn't told my agent about—or April. Just like April had once told me, maybe I needed to ride the chaos.

I hoped I was ready for a new beginning, good and free of trouble. But I couldn't lie to myself about the biggest secret I still harbored: I would never propose to April Forrest. It would be too cruel to inflict someone like me on a nice girl like her.

"I want to see you," my mouth told April, ignoring my conviction. "I miss you."

This time, the silence was barely noticeable. "I know, Ten," she said. "I miss you, too."

The story continues in *South by Southeast*, available in September 2012 in paperback and eBook from ATRIA BOOKS.

About Atria Books

Atria Books was launched in April 2002 by publisher Judith Curr as a new hardcover and paperback imprint within Simon & Schuster, Inc. The name Atria (the plural of atrium—a central living space open to the air and sky) reflects our goals as publishers: to create an environment that is always open to new ideas and where our authors and their books can flourish. We look for innovative ways to connect writers and readers, integrating the best practices of traditional publishing with the latest innovations in the digital world. We are committed to publishing a wide range of fiction and nonfiction for readers of all tastes and interests.

The first book published under the Atria name, *The Right Words at the Right Time* by Marlo Thomas, became an instant #1 *New York Times* bestseller, and since then Atria has gone on to publish more than 185 *New York Times* bestsellers. Atria is the publishing home to many major bestselling authors, including His Holiness the Dalai Lama, Jude Deveraux, Vince Flynn, T.D. Jakes, Shirley MacLaine, Kate Morton, Jodi Picoult, Sister Souljah, Brad Thor, Jennifer Weiner, Lauren Weisberger, Zane, and Rhonda Byrne, author of the international bestsellers *The Secret* and *The Power*.

In recent years, the imprint has placed a strategic emphasis on publishing for diverse audiences through the acquisition of the African American–oriented press Strebor Books, the launch of Atria Books Español, and copublishing agreements with Beyond Words Publishers and Cash Money Records. Atria Books also publishes literary fiction and topical nonfiction in trade paperback under the Washington Square Press imprint, and popular fiction and nonfiction under the Emily Bestler Books imprint, launched in 2011.

Atria—books that entertain and enlighten.

ABOUT EMILY BESTLER BOOKS

Remember the first time you fell in love with a book? We hope to recapture that feeling for you over and over. Emily Bestler Books was founded with one guiding principle in mind: to find the very best reads available and to put them into the hands of as many readers as we can. We are passionate about this mission and in pursuit of it have decided to give ourselves as much leeway as possible and open the imprint up to a number of different categories. After all, books are as varied as their readers. On our shelves you will find fiction and nonfiction, pulse-pounding thrillers, delectable cookbooks, distinctive memoirs, international crime fiction, and smart, deeply felt novels with a literary flair. In short, we have a book for everyone.

EMILY
BESTLER
BOOKS

ABOUT WASHINGTON SQUARE PRESS

Since becoming part of Simon & Schuster in 1959, Washington Square Press's mission has been to bring the best in contemporary and classic literature to the widest readership possible. Upon Atria's founding in 2002, WSP became the trade paperback home of some of America's most talented contemporary storytellers, including Jodi Picoult, Jennifer Weiner, and Kate Morton, joining such WSP backlist luminaries as Pearl Buck, Carlos Castaneda, Jim Harrison, Walter Mosley, and Wally Lamb.

WASHINGTON SQUARE PRESS